THE ROSE

Meg held out both her hands. In one, there was a small note. In the other, there was a pile of rose petals. "I found this in your Secret Note place," Meg said.

Laura took the note, opened it, and read: *"Hi."* It was signed simply, *"Rose."*

"The Rose!" Laura said in shock. "It must be that girl! But how does she know where I live? How does she know where my hiding place is? Why is she bothering me like this?"

P.S. We'll Miss You
Yours 'Til the Meatball Bounces
2 Sweet 2 B 4-Gotten
Remember Me, When This You See
Sealed with a Hug
Friends 'Til the Ocean Waves
Friends 4-Ever Minus One
Mysteriously Yours

MYSTERIOUSLY YOURS

Deirdre Corey

AN
APPLE
PAPERBACK

SCHOLASTIC INC.
New York Toronto London Auckland Sydney

ISBN 0-590-44030-6

12 11 10 9 8 7 6 5 4 3 2 1   1 2 3 4 5 6/9

Printed in the U.S.A.   40

First Scholastic printing, June 1991

For
H.A.

CELEBRATION DAY

Stevie Ames stood up, waving excitedly. Her reddish-blonde hair looked as wild as her arms flapping above her head, and for once she wore a T-shirt and skirt instead of jeans.

"Stevie!" said Laura breathlessly. "How'd you get here from Miss Humphrey's studio so fast?"

"You two look incredible!" gasped Stevie before answering Laura's question. She stepped back to get a better look at her two friends still in their costumes and stage makeup. Laura, of course, looked like she belonged in the free-flowing, filmy costume. It was as delicate as she was. Molly, on the other hand, looked beautiful but incomplete without her usual cowgirl boots on her feet. Still, Stevie couldn't get over how glamorous they both looked up close. "Incredible!" she said again.

Laura was dressed in a beautiful, rose-colored satin tunic with pink tights and a flowing rose-colored cape. Molly wore a gauzy, rainbow tunic and cape that fell in layers of different-colored chiffon. Both girls were fully made-up with dark pink lipstick, blusher, and eyeshadow all the way up to their pencil-darkened eyebrows. And the crowning touch, bobby-pinned to the tops of each head, was a rhinestone tiara.

"So how *did* you get here so fast?" Laura asked again, smoothing out the satin cape and sitting down at the table.

"Oh," answered Stevie, plopping down in her seat without straightening her skirt. "My mom dropped us off while she and the other moms went to park the car. I just ran in and grabbed a table for us and one for our moms."

"Where's Meg?" Laura wondered, looking around the crowded little restaurant. She saw lots of girls she knew. Shana McCardle's spiky black hair made her easy to spot over at a table across the room. She waved at Laura and flashed a V for victory sign as she shouted across the room.

2

"You were great, Laura!"

"Thanks, Shana," Laura called back. She still didn't see Meg. Next her eyes fell on the two Know-It-Alls, Suzi Taylor and Erica Soames. Of course they *had* to be here where all the recital celebrating was going on. They were probably writing articles for their silly newspaper, *The Gifted Express*. Both of them had tried out for leading roles in the ballet program, but for once Friends 4-Ever topped the Know-It-Alls two to nothing. Laura and Molly won the main parts. All that was left for Erica and Suzi to do was to act like they were star reporters getting the scoop on the big ballet show. Now that Meg wasn't in the Gifted Program anymore, Laura didn't care at all if she and Molly were written up in that newspaper.

"Where *is* Meg?" Laura asked again. In the crowd she still didn't see the bouncy blonde curls of her friend anywhere.

Stevie pushed her flyaway hair out of her blue eyes. One strand caught in the corner of her mouth, and she talked for a second with it still there. "Meg's over at the Mothers' Table getting money for the jukebox."

Then she felt the hair in her mouth. "Ptooey!" she said, as she pulled the strand away. "I swear I'm gonna cut this mop off one of these days."

"I'll cut it for you, Stevie," Meg Milano's voice said behind her. "Give me a knife. I'm experienced at cutting hair."

The girls all laughed knowingly. They remembered very well the day Meg had cut off one of her own curls to send to Molly when Molly lived in Kansas.

Meg lifted up Stevie's straggly hair and twisted it into a knotted ponytail.

"Cut it out!" said Stevie, pulling her hair back from Meg.

"Oh, I thought you wanted me to cut it *off*," joked Meg as she dropped the handful of hair and headed for the jukebox. "My mother gave me fifty cents. Don't worry. I'll pick songs we all like." Meg marched off, sure as usual that she knew exactly what everyone else would like.

"Slow songs," voted Laura.

"Fast," called out Stevie.

"Both," said Molly, always the one to see both sides of every argument.

As the girls got settled in their seats, their mothers waved from a table across the room and went on talking. That was fine with the girls. They liked sitting at a table by themselves. And they especially liked ordering whatever they wanted from the menu. Since today was a special celebration day all their mothers had given permission to have anything and everything.

Meg returned to the table just as a slow song started to play on the jukebox. "Can I try on your crown?" she asked Laura. "Please? I played a slow song especially for you."

"Here," said Molly, before Laura had a chance to take her own tiara off. "Take mine." She reached up and unpinned her crown from her short brown hair. "It slides around too much on me, anyway. My hair isn't as thick as Laura's. It doesn't hold the bobby pins so well."

"It still looks beautiful on you," Stevie said.

"Want to try it?" Molly asked, laughing.

"On *you* I said," Stevie replied, putting her hands up to protect her head from such an un-Stevie-like thing as a glittering crown. "That's not exactly my style of hat."

"Mine either, really," agreed Molly. "I'd rather be wearing a cowboy hat."

All the girls giggled as they passed the tiara around and finally turned their attention to the emerald-green menus. Stevie held hers upside down for two whole minutes before anyone even noticed.

"Oh!" she said, faking surprise when Meg pointed it out to her. "I was trying to figure out

5

what a 'tilps ananab' was." She turned the menu the right way. "Aha!" she realized aloud. "It's 'banana split.' That's what I'm having," Stevie told the waitress, who had come to take their orders.

"How can you, Stevie?" gasped Laura, holding her stomach. "I could never eat all that. I think I'll just have the raspberry sherbet with the wafer cookie on top." The waitress wrote down Laura's order.

"Hey, we're celebrating here, and you're the star! Is sherbet enough?" Meg looked over the menu and then announced that she was having a chocolate float.

"And I'll have a Purple Cow," said Molly, choosing the grape-soda-and-vanilla-ice-cream drink and handing over her menu to the waitress.

"Only because they don't have a Purple *Horse*," Stevie teased. They all knew that horses were everything to Molly.

Although the restaurant was filled with happy recital celebrators, none of the tables seemed quite as jolly as the table with the four Friends 4-Ever. Anyone watching would have seen that these four girls were the best of friends. The way they laughed together, teased each other, and complimented each other was proof to any on-looker that these four would be friends forever.

The girls had all grown up together in their neighborhood of Crispin Landing in Camden, Rhode Island. For as long as they could remember they had shared all kinds of experiences, from nursery school, to camp, to clubs of all kinds, to the terrible day when Molly announced she was moving to Kansas for a year. While long distance might have broken up another friendship, the move only seemed to strengthen the relationship among the girls.

"Don't say it," said Molly, looking up from her menu. "I know what you're thinking."

"What?" said Stevie, trying to look innocent.

"You're thinking I should have ordered something chocolate since my friend's horse in Kansas is named Chocolate," Molly said.

"Well, that's only because you usually do order chocolate, and then you talk about Chocolate for the next fifteen minutes." Stevie laughed as she said this.

Of the four friends, Molly was Stevie's best best friend. And both girls had a knack for knowing what the other was thinking before either one said a word. The same went for Meg and Laura.

"Today I'm not talking about chocolate or Chocolate," said Molly. "There's too much other stuff to talk about."

"You mean the announcement Miss Humphrey made after the recital?" asked Laura. "Can you believe we're going to get the chance to repeat our performance at the new Crispin Mansion?"

"A charity luncheon, and we're going to be the entertainment! It's so fabulous!" said Molly. "I've always been curious about what was inside that big house Mrs. Crispin lives in. Now we'll get to see it, and we'll meet Mrs. Crispin!"

"I can hardly wait!" exclaimed Laura. "It's going to be so great."

"For you and Molly, maybe," said Stevie jealously. "But what about Meg and me? How are we going to get in on the big event? We want to see that mansion, too. The Crispin family must be zillionaires to live in a place that humongous!"

"I don't think they're zillionaires," said Meg. "But they are the oldest and richest family around here. They used to own our whole neighborhood until Mr. Crispin died."

"Good thing they moved to the other side of town," said Stevie. "If they hadn't sold all that property, our houses would never have been built."

"And if our houses had never been built, we might not have all lived so close to each other," continued Molly.

"And if we didn't all live so close to each other . . ." Laura started.

"We would have found each other anyway, and we would have still been best friends," finished Meg matter-of-factly. "But anyway, I sure would like to get a look at that place. It's only about ten times as big as the house they moved from."

"I don't know about *that*," disagreed Molly. "The *old* Crispin house is pretty huge. I've never gone through the iron gates to get a real close-up look, but the top of the house sticks out way past the trees around it."

"I've always thought it was kind of spooky," said Laura. "That's why I've never gone near it."

"Well, with that old graveyard in the back, it's no wonder!" said Stevie. "Just peeking through the bushes and seeing those crumbling tombstones is enough to give anyone the creeps. I can see why they moved!"

"And because of that graveyard they never sold the house," said Meg.

"Yeah, and who would buy a house with a graveyard, anyway? Maybe the *Addams Family* or the *Munsters* from TV," laughed Stevie.

"Hey," said Laura. "Don't forget that my family bought our house, and it has a part of the Crispin gatehouse on it. Our whole porch is left over from the original gatehouse."

"Well, that's not the same thing as having tombstones in your yard," Meg argued.

Just then the waitress came with a tray full of delicious-looking treats. "Purple Cow," she said, setting the tall, foaming drink down in front of Molly. "Banana split?"

"Right here," said Stevie, already holding her spoon in the ready-to-dig-in position.

"Sherbet, and chocolate float?" asked the waitress.

"Here for the float," said Meg, "and there for the sherbet," she said, pointing to Laura's place.

For the moment, the girls put aside their discussion about the Crispin Mansion and turned their attention to the celebration feast.

Stevie held up a heaping spoonful of chocolate ice cream dripping with marshmallow topping. "Here's to our two stars 4-Ever, Laura and Molly, for dancing their way into the hearts of millions!"

"And into the home of a millionaire," Meg added, taking a slurp of her chocolate float.

With the jukebox playing Meg's selection of songs in the background, Laura, Meg, Molly, and Stevie spent the next half hour toasting each other, toasting their friendship, and toasting their toasting. Through all the laughter and celebration the girls also sang along with the songs. Meg and Laura even got up and danced a little right by the table. Even Stevie stood up and pretended to be wild on the dance floor, but just for a second.

"Hey, look!" Stevie called out, when they'd all sat back down. She pointed to Laura's gleaming tiara. "It's sparkling in the light. It looks like some magic spell has been put on you or something!"

"Oh, yeah," Molly said, seeing what Stevie meant. "The way the light is catching the rhinestones, there's almost a halo around your head."

Laura turned her head to one side, trying to see what they were talking about. "I can't see it," she said, turning the other way.

"There!" said Meg. "Stay still! Hold your head just that way. Perfect."

Laura sat statue-still with her head turned to one side and her eyes turned upwards. She looked like some beautiful angel with the

11

diamond-lights twinkling around her soft cloud of hair.

"Don't move!" Stevie reminded her, as Laura started to change her position.

As her friends were getting a good look from every angle, they didn't notice what Laura did. Standing as frozen as Laura sat, a girl about her age stared at Laura as though the lights around Laura's head had hypnotized her.

Laura still didn't move. She stared back at the strange girl. Laura tried to figure out what it was that made this girl seem different. She wore round, tortoiseshell glasses. But lots of kids wore glasses. Nothing strange about that. Maybe it was her pale white complexion that made her skin look almost as if it were marble. Or maybe it was the way her hair was so perfectly cut straight across at earlobe level. It was such a dark brown color that it was almost black. Holding the hair on one side was an old-fashioned-style bow made of rose-colored satin. In fact, it was the same color as Laura's costume.

Now, that's strange, thought Laura.

The dark-haired girl still didn't move. Neither did Laura. As Laura sat under her halo of lights, the girl seemed almost caught in a dreamlike spotlight of her own. Her flowered dress, pale pink tights, and white patent-leather party shoes gave the girl the look of a bouquet of flowers. It was that thought that made Laura suddenly aware of the fact that the girl really was holding a flower.

Now the girl started to slowly move toward Laura.

"Look," Laura barely whispered to her friends who were still busy buzzing about the lights and the halo and the diamonds sparkling. She still hadn't moved.

"Look!" Laura said again, louder this time.

Now, one by one her friends' attention turned to the girl who moved stiffly toward Laura. "Who is she?" asked Meg.

"Why is she coming over to us?" Stevie wondered.

"She isn't coming over to us," corrected Molly. "She's coming over to *Laura*. Do you know her, Laura?"

Laura still didn't budge. She sat still as could be, watching the girl getting closer and closer. Taking one more step toward the table, the girl said nothing as she held out the one single rose.

At first, Laura didn't take it. The girl held it closer and finally just placed it on the table in front of Laura. Then she turned and hurried through the crowd and disappeared somewhere in the back of the restaurant where Emerald City was painted on the wall.

"Whew! Weird!" said Stevie. "Wasn't that weird?"

Laura picked up the rose. It was the same color as her costume and as the girl's hair bow.

"Nice flower, though," said Molly. "I've never seen one that color before."

"Are you all right, Laura?" Meg asked, suddenly noticing that Laura looked frightened.

"I'm not sure," said Laura. "I mean, nothing really happened, but for some reason I just feel kind of creepy."

"And with good reason," said Stevie. "She was like a ghost-girl or something. Was she real or what?"

"Oh, she was real, all right," said Meg. "Real strange, that is."

"A real mystery, you mean," Molly added.

The word *mystery* snapped Laura out of her trance. She turned her head toward her friends quickly and said, "That's it! I've got it!"

"Got what?" asked Meg.

"A rose," answered Stevie.

"And a great idea," said Laura, her eyes sparkling almost as much as her jeweled tiara. "Let's bring back the Clue Club we used to have. Only this time, instead of making up mysteries to solve, we'll solve a real one. The Mystery of The Rose!"

Molly picked up the rose and turned it over between two fingers. "It really is a strange one," she said. "The color is very unusual."

"And so is the girl who delivered it," said Laura.

"Why was she just staring at you like that?" Stevie asked.

"And where did she come from?" Molly said, putting the flower down.

"And where did she disappear to?" Meg said mysteriously.

"And why did she leave the rose?" Stevie said in her own mysterious voice.

"The Clue Club is now officially reformed," Meg said, tapping her knuckles on the table.

Now Laura picked up the rose and turned it between her two fingers. As she did, she was surprised by a sharp pain in her finger. "Ouch!" she said, throwing the rose down on the table and quickly putting her pricked finger in her mouth. "A thorn, I guess," she explained.

"Don't put your finger in your mouth!" screamed Molly. "It might be poisoned!"

The three girls laughed at Molly's overly dramatic reaction. Laura let her head fall backwards as she whispered her last words, "The Clue Club must solve the Mystery of The Rose!" Laura closed her eyes and slumped in her chair.

"Laura!" screamed Molly.

"What?" asked Laura, sitting up normally and adjusting her tiara.

Now all the girls laughed. Even Molly. But Laura brought things back to a serious note when she repeated, "The Mystery of The Rose. Hmmm. And the only clue we have is the rose."

"I propose a toast to the biggest mystery the Clue Club has ever had," said Meg, raising her chocolate float glass in the air.

"To The Rose!" added Stevie, lifting a spoonful of marshmallow topping.

"To The Rose!" said Laura and Molly together.

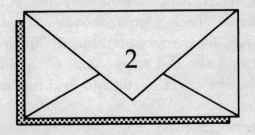

THE CLUE CLUB

Sitting on her bed alone in her room, with the rose-colored costume spread out neatly beside her, Laura stared at the rose, which she'd laid on top of her costume. The colors matched exactly. Ever since the day before, Laura had been trying to shake off a feeling she could only describe as "creepy."

When she really thought about it, she guessed there was nothing that strange about what had happened at the Yellow Brick Road restaurant. All her friends were excited about the way the ceiling lights were reflecting off her rhinestone tiara. They saw it, and probably that strange girl saw it, too. So what? So why did she just walk toward Laura without saying a word? And why did she give Laura the rose? And why did the girl look like she was from a different century? Her flowered dress and the way she wore her hair pinned back with that rose-colored bow made her look so old-fashioned. She almost looked as if she had stepped out of an old photograph. She stood so still and held that rose so carefully.

Remembering the feeling of being pricked by the thorn, Laura once again put her sore finger up to her lips and held it there. She sat like that for a moment. The ring of the telephone brought her thoughts back to the present. Jumping up from her bed, Laura ran to the telephone table in the hallway and picked up the phone.

"Hello?" she said. No answer. "Hello?" Laura said again. No answer again. She put the receiver back in place. "Wrong number, I guess," she said aloud.

As she turned to go back into her room, the phone rang again. This time Laura picked up the phone and started talking right away. "What number are you calling?" she asked, sounding a little annoyed.

"*Your* number," said Meg's voice on the other end.

"Oh, it's you, Meg!" laughed Laura.

"'Oh, it's you, Meg' you say. Of course it's me. I told you I'd call you at ten o'clock and it's ten o'clock. Who else would it be?" Meg was teasing Laura, and Laura didn't mind.

"No," she said. "I wasn't expecting it to be anyone else. So what did you decide? Are we having our first Clue Club meeting at your house?"

"Can't," said Meg. "My mother's having a book group meeting with a bunch of ladies coming over, so she said no."

"What about Stevie's house?" Laura asked, holding the phone under her chin as she pointed one toe gracefully out to the side and reached down with her arm to "gather the flowers," as Miss Humphrey would say.

"Stevie's house is out, too," Meg replied. "Her mom will be out showing a house so nobody will be home."

"And Molly?" Laura went down the Friends 4-Ever list.

"When I asked her she said, 'Are you kidding? With Scotty here?' Her brother's having two other six-year-olds over today so Molly said her house will be like a zoo." Meg laughed.

"So I guess my house is it. My mom isn't working at the bookstore today." Laura sighed.

"We'll just have to squeeze into my tiny room as best as we can, that's all." She dragged the phone from the hallway into her room. As she spoke, she looked around her room. She saw the autographed ballet shoes hanging on her pale pink wall. All her other ballet things were hung neatly on a white clothes rack. The single bed with its pink-and-white-dotted-swiss bedspread practically filled the whole room. It left just enough space for a tiny white dresser and matching desk. Laura liked her room. But it was definitely too tiny to be the regular Clue Club meeting place.

"I'll call the others and tell them we'll meet at your house, okay?" Meg volunteered.

"Great," said Laura.

"And Laura?" Meg added slowly.

"Yes?" said Laura.

"Remember The Rose!" Meg spoke in her most mysterious-sounding voice.

"How could I forget it?" asked Laura. "I *have* it!"

The two friends said good-bye, and Laura put the phone back on the table in the hallway. She did one more toe-point to the side, one more sweeping of her arm to the floor, and then went back into her room. Looking around her tiny room again, Laura sighed. "Hopeless," she said to herself. And then as a thought came to her she said aloud, "Maybe not."

Immediately Laura began moving the few pieces of furniture around. She'd tried this many times before and always thought that the room might somehow magically grow if the furniture were rearranged the right way. It didn't. In fact, what had always happened before, happened again this time. The bed, the dresser, and the desk went right back to where they had been in the first place. Laura's mother was right. This arrangement really was the best one.

Laura was just putting everything back when the girls arrived.

"Come on up!" Laura called out when she heard their voices downstairs.

Meg led the way up the narrow staircase. "Ready or not, here we come!" Meg called back.

"Squeeze in," joked Laura, pressing her thin figure up against the wall and sucking in her breath.

"Oh, Laura," laughed Molly. "Your room isn't *that* small."

"In fact, it's just right," said Stevie. "Since we only have one clue it's not like we need a whole warehouse to store them all."

21

"What I think," said Meg, "is that we should find a regular place to meet. Some place that is all ours whether there's a silly book group meeting or little brothers around or nobody home or whatever. You know. A place that is really a clubhouse."

"Hey," said Stevie, getting a bright idea. "My mother's in the real estate business. Maybe she's got a listing for a clubhouse for sale!"

"Funny, Stevie. Very funny," Meg said, not laughing.

"Well, what do you really mean, Meg?" asked Laura.

"I mean we should spend this first meeting finding a place for our second meeting and for all the meetings after that," Meg explained patiently.

"Why don't we go exploring around the neighborhood?" suggested Stevie. "We'll search high and low. And I'll take the high since I know every branch of every tree in Crispin Landing."

"We're *not* meeting up in a tree!" said Meg, horrified at the thought of having to climb a tree every time they met.

"But exploring is a great idea," Molly said, rescuing some of Stevie's idea.

"Let's go!" Laura exclaimed excitedly. She was

glad to have the chance to lead everyone out of her cramped quarters. The girls followed her down the stairs. Each walked in her own special way. Laura glided gracefully down the stairs with her dancers' feet barely touching the steps.

Next, Meg bounced behind Laura, her blonde curls boinging against her head with each step.

Molly, of course, galloped with a clip-clop sound all the way down the stairs.

And Stevie sat sidesaddle on the railing, sliding the whole way down and landing on her feet with a thud at the bottom.

Once they were outside, they realized they didn't really know where they were going. "Let's just start walking and see where we end up," Stevie suggested, taking the lead. "We don't have to plan *everything*, do we?" She walked past the log cabin birdhouse that hung in the tree in Laura's front yard. The other girls followed.

"Wait," said Laura, stopping by the birdhouse and reaching her hand into the chimney. "Let me just see if there are any Secret Note Society messages for me today." She felt around in the chimney and pulled out a small, folded note. "Hey! A note!"

Meg had a big smile on her face as they all watched Laura unfold the paper. In a second they could all see the familiar kittens on the border of the paper. This was Meg's special stationery.

"Remember The Rose!" Laura read out loud. "Ugh, not again!"

"Just kidding," said Meg. "But at least I left a note."

They had all been leaving notes for each other in their separate Secret Note Society hiding places ever since Molly had moved back home from Kansas. Writing down their thoughts and ideas was a habit they'd gotten into when they used to write back and forth from Rhode Island to Kansas. They had each chosen their own special stationery — kittens for Meg, rainbows for Molly, high-top sneakers for Stevie, and unicorns for Laura. Now they used that same stationery for the notes.

"Thanks, Meg," Laura said, folding the note back up and stuffing it into the pocket of her purple pants. Leaving the birdhouse swinging on the branch, Laura and the other Clue Club members went in search of the perfect meeting place.

The girls walked across Crispin Landing, the main street that ran through the neighborhood and the street on which Laura lived. As they turned down Half Moon Lane, where both Stevie and Molly lived, Stevie ran ahead and jumped up onto one of the lower branches of her favorite tree. As Laura had done with the birdhouse chimney, Stevie reached into a hollow in the tree. She pulled out a folded note.

"Hey! I got a secret note!" she said, surprised to find one since they were all together and a note wasn't really needed. She unfolded it and rainbows appeared showing that it was a note from Molly. *"Remember The Rose!"* Stevie read.

"I swear," said Molly. "I didn't know Meg was writing the same thing to Laura. It's just a coincidence."

"It just shows we're all on the same wavelength," Meg explained in her sensible way.

"Want to come up and have a meeting up here?" Stevie called down from a branch so high up the girls on the ground had to shade their eyes to find her. "The view is incredible, and we could probably find all the clues in the world with a good pair of binoculars."

"Come on down," Molly cried, sounding worried. "You're too high."

"No, really," said Stevie. "I can see everything! I've never been up *this* far before."

"Stevie, please come down!" Laura called up to their daring friend.

"Hey! I can even see into the old Crispin estate! You're not going to believe this! There's another house behind the big house!" Stevie stood on her tiptoes so she could see even more. "No," she corrected herself. "It's not a house. I think it's a barn or something. If I climb just one branch higher I can really see."

Just as her friends all screamed out, "Don't!" Stevie reached her foot up to a small branch. The branch snapped off and went tumbling down through the branches below it. Stevie screamed as she teetered, but quickly caught her balance and steadied herself as she held tightly to another branch.

"Stevie!" screamed the girls below. Was their friend going to follow the falling branch?

"No sweat," laughed Stevie nervously as she did her usual monkey-swing down from branch to branch. "Ta da!" she sang, landing in an Olympic winner's pose with her arms raised in a V.

"Stevie Ames!" scolded Laura. "You had us all scared to death!"

"When that branch came falling down I was sure it was all over for you!" Molly gasped.

"Well, that's just one more great reason why we aren't going to have our meetings up in any old tree!" Meg said triumphantly. "Trees are for birds and squirrels, and the only nuts up in a tree should be the ones the squirrels bring!"

"Hey!" said Stevie, acting hurt. "Who are you calling a nut?"

"If the shell fits, wear it," Meg said with a laugh. "Just *kidding*."

"Well, anyway," Stevie continued as if she *hadn't* just given her three best friends a terrible scare, "you should see what I saw up there. You won't believe it! How could all that be back there and we don't even know about it?"

"What are you talking about, Stevie?" Laura asked. "Back where?"

"Behind the old Crispin Mansion. Didn't you hear me yell down that there's a barn back there? The trees have grown so high around the old place that we haven't seen the half of it," Stevie said excitedly. *"That's* where we should be exploring."

"The old Crispin house?" Laura whispered. "You mean go inside the gate?"

"Why not?" said Stevie. "It's like a whole other world back there. It's not just a graveyard. There are gardens and statues and everything. You wouldn't believe it!"

"Let's take a vote," Meg suggested, always choosing the practical solution to every problem.

"All in favor of going exploring at the old Crispin Mansion raise your hand." She raised her own.

Stevie's hand shot up in a yes vote.

Molly's hand followed, but not quite so quickly.

Laura looked around at the three hands in the air, gave a big sigh, and slowly raised her own hand with the others. "Well, all right," she said. "But I'm holding on to you, Meg. I'm not getting lost in there with all those tombstones and overgrown vines."

"Remember The Rose!" reminded Stevie. "We need a place to meet to solve our mystery, right? Maybe we'll find the perfect place right there. Let's go!" She started running ahead, and the others followed close behind.

Stevie ran down the sidewalk, past Molly's house and through Molly's backyard. As the other girls caught up, Molly yelled out, "Wait! Let me check my Secret Note spot!" She reached over to the knotted fringe on the striped hammock that hung between two trees in her backyard. Sure enough, there was a note. This one had a pair of blue high-top sneakers at the top of the page. It was from Stevie.

"Ha!" laughed Molly. "Guess what it says?"

"Remember The Rose?" guessed Laura.

"What else?" said Molly, giggling.

"Of course," Stevie said. "Now, let's go. We can cut through the path and come out on Meg's street. Come on!" She was off and running again.

Molly galloped after her, Meg bounced her way through the bushes, and Laura leaped through the air like a deer. Coming out on Double-tree Court, the explorers made one last stop in front of Meg's house. It was Meg's turn to find her secret note left in a knothole of the fence post closest to her front door. As she unfolded the paper, the unicorns that she expected to see were across the top. It was from Laura, of course, and the message was no surprise to any of them.

" 'Remember The Rose!' " Meg read. "You've got to admit we really do think alike," she said, stuffing the note into her jeans pocket. "And what we're all thinking about is The Rose!"

"Well, right now what I'm thinking about is getting inside those gates at the Crispin estate," Stevie said, reminding them all where they were headed.

"Hey," Molly said, realizing something for the first time. "If there's a barn, maybe there are horses!"

"Well, they'd be ghosts of horses by now,"

laughed Stevie. "Nobody's lived there for years."

"Oh, I mean maybe there's horse stuff in the barn," Molly corrected herself, seeing how what she'd said sounded so silly.

"If it even is a barn," Laura added. "You said you weren't sure what it was, right, Stevie?"

"True. Just as I was about to get a better look, the breaking branch changed my plans. But we're about to find out for sure." Stevie led the group through Meg's backyard, across another street, around a corner, and through a small common area where people mostly just walked their dogs. On the other side of the grassy area was a wall of thick, overgrown hedges with another wall of tall evergreen trees behind it. A person really had to know that there was a house behind all the bushes and trees to even bother looking for a gate. Stevie had seen exactly where the gate was from her spot high up in the tree.

"Are you sure it's here?" Laura asked in a frightened whisper. "Oh, I don't think this is such a good idea."

"I do," said Meg, making her way to the front of the group. "Come on, help Stevie and me move these vines out of the way. There's definitely a gate behind them. I can see the latch.

There's a padlock on it, but it's just hanging open!" Meg was excitedly pulling long, brittle vines away from what they could all soon see was a big iron-barred gate.

"The padlock isn't the only thing open," shrieked Molly. "The whole gate's open. All that's keeping it closed is this tangled mess of vines!"

The girls tugged and pulled at the vines until they were able to push the heavy, iron gate open wide enough for them to slip through. "We made it!" Stevie gasped.

"Sshhh!" said Laura. "Listen!"

The girls stood quietly, listening for what Laura had heard. They heard it, too. Silence. There were no sounds of cars or kids or dogs barking or any of the usual noises of Crispin Landing. The walls of overgrowth were so thick and high, all the sounds of the outside world were kept out.

"It's so peaceful," whispered Molly. "Like a fairyland or something."

"It doesn't seem *too* spooky," agreed Laura, looking up the long, curving, stone walkway that led to the towering mansion. "Isn't it beautiful?"

"Why would the Crispins ever want to leave a huge house like this?" Stevie wondered aloud.

"To move to an even huger one," Meg answered. "But this one is like something out of a book. Look at the round towers. Even the windows are curved. Let's get a closer look!"

"Where's the graveyard?" Laura asked, not really wanting to know. "If it's this quiet here, just imagine how quiet it must be there." Laura turned to look back to the side of the house. "I don't see anything on that side," she said. "Meg! Are you really going up to the house?"

Meg was already starting up the stone walkway. Stevie left the path and ran ahead to where another walkway led around to the other side of the house.

"You guys!" Molly called out. "Wait for us! Come on, Laura," she added, pulling Laura by the arm.

"Well, let's follow Meg, okay?" Laura said. "I'd rather stay to the front of the house instead of going around to the side. I don't want to suddenly be standing on a bunch of graves."

Just then Stevie's voice called out from around the side of the house. "Hey, everyone," she shouted. "Come here! Wait'll you see this!"

All the girls hurried over to where Stevie was standing on tiptoe peering into a long, beveled glass window with roses etched in the glass.

"What a beautiful window!" Laura exclaimed. Then, "Look! The Rose!"

"Oh, yeah," said Meg, noticing the etchings in the glass. "Isn't that a coincidence?"

"Never mind that," Stevie interrupted them. "Look at what I'm looking at. It's a bedroom and there's a closet and the closet's open and there's a — "

"Let us look!" Molly stopped her, as she moved up to the window and stood on tiptoe, too. "Oh my gosh! There are dresses in the closet. Old dresses. Aren't they beautiful?"

"Well, you're definitely right that they're old," Stevie said, not really seeing the beauty in a bunch of old dresses. "And so is that big canopy bed."

Molly moved aside and let Laura and Meg have a look. She walked around to the back of the house while the others talked more about the clothes, the bed, and the shelves of books that lined the walls of the room. And next it was Molly's voice calling that brought all the girls running to the back of the house.

"The barn!" Molly cried out happily. "Isn't it so incredible? It reminds me of my friend Kristy in Kansas. She had a barn in back of her house, too."

"This is too unbelievable," said Stevie excitedly. "Let's go in. The door is open."

All four of the girls held on to each others' shirts or arms or hands as they carefully pulled the big barn door open wider. As the door opened and they filed in, a streak of sunlight followed them, lighting the barn enough for them to see that it had four stalls, piles of hay all around, and a stairway leading to another floor of the building. Stevie led the way up the stairs.

When they all reached the last step and stood together in the hayloft it seemed as if they all had the exact same idea at the same time. "Our new Clue Club meeting place!" Meg was the first to say it, but the others all insisted that they were just about to say the same thing.

"It's perfect," Laura said.

"It even smells perfect," Molly agreed, breathing the scent of horses that still filled the old barn. "And look, there really *are* horse things here!" She held up an old bridle, a couple of horseshoes, and some horseshoe nails.

Then Meg laughed. "Laura," she said, "you're doing it again."

"I know, I know," said Laura, laughing, too. "I guess I just can't help myself." Just as she had rearranged the furniture in her room, she was already busy moving the bales of hay that were neatly stacked. Laura made seats and a big table out of the tightly packed hay rectangles. "There!" she said, brushing loose bits of hay from her hands and the front of her flowered T-shirt.

Meg kicked a small pile of hay aside and made her own discovery. It was a pile of rusty old tools. She bent down and picked up an old hammer. Stepping forward, hammer in hand, Meg tapped it on the hay table Laura had made. "Attention, attention!" Meg announced. "All those in favor of claiming this space as our new Clue Club Clubhouse, say 'Aye.'"

Four "Aye's" made it a done deal. Meg tapped the hammer again. "The barn is hereby declared the official Clue Club meeting place. Our pledge is that we shall always be dedicated to truth, justice, and the Friends-4-Ever way!"

"Yes!" said Stevie, laying her hand down flat on the hay table.

"Agreed," Molly said, adding her hand to Stevie's.

"Friends 4-Ever," said Meg, topping the pile of hands with her own.

"Forever," Laura whispered as she gently

placed her hand with the others. Looking around at her three friends, Laura knew that this was one pledge she would always keep. "Forever," she said again.

The friends squeezed hands, and began their first Clue Club meeting in their new Clue Club Clubhouse.

THE SLEEPOVER

The secret meeting place in the hayloft of the old barn was changed from a hay-covered storage area into a hay-covered club room with a view of the old Crispin Mansion and the once-beautiful gardens surrounding it. The girls spent the rest of the first meeting setting up the "room." Meg and Molly ran home to get paper, pencils, and other club supplies. Stevie's last words to them as they ran out the big barn door were, "Get snacks!"

"Don't worry," Laura assured Stevie as she

pulled her head back inside the big hayloft window, "Meg will remember everything. She always does."

Stevie stuck her head out the window again. "Look around out here, Laura!" she said to the outside.

"What?" Laura asked, as she struggled with another bale of hay to add to the ones she'd lined up to make a "couch."

Stevie pulled her head in again. "Come and look out here. I can see the graveyard."

"You can?" Laura said, coming up beside Stevie and looking for herself. "Oh yeah, way over there behind the garden with the statues. It isn't a very big graveyard, is it? What's that big building in the middle of it?"

"Let's go over there," Stevie said daringly.

"But what if Meg and Molly come back and they don't know where we are?" Laura worried.

"We'll leave a note," Stevie said.

"On what? We have no paper," Laura pointed out.

"Right here," Stevie said, picking up a screwdriver off the pile of rusty tools. On the floor in the middle of their meeting area, Stevie scratched a message in the dust.

Gone to graveyard. Back soon. S. & L.

"There," said Stevie, laying the screwdriver down by the message. "That should do it. Let's go."

The two girls walked down the rustic staircase and went out the barn door. Turning to the right, they took the stone path that led to the sculptured gardens behind the main house. The path wound around in a circle and in the center there was a marble statue of a girl wearing a wreath of marble roses around her head. All the bushes around the statue were brown and broken, but it was clear that once this had been a beautiful rose garden.

"She must have been Queen of the Roses," Laura said dreamily, stopping to look at the statue and imagining herself in its place.

"Well she's Queen of the *Dead* Roses now," said Stevie as she followed the path to the place where the small graveyard began.

The stones that marked the graves were old. Some of them were crumbling so that the names and dates could hardly be read. Stevie and Laura walked slowly on the dirt path that was in front of each stone. They tried to read where they could.

"Louise Crispin, Wife of Ethan Crispin, 1823–1858," Laura read. "Gosh, she was so young!"

"Look at this one!" Stevie called from another stone farther up the path. *"Sarah Elizabeth Crispin, born September 3, 1856, died September 7, 1856."*

"Oh, how terrible," cried Laura. "She was just a baby!" Laura felt tears filling her eyes as she and Stevie continued along the path reading the names of all the Crispins and some other gravestones with the family name of Pearce. When they came to the building in the middle of the graveyard they could now see that it was a family crypt with the Crispin name etched in the marble over the doorway. A wrought-iron door was open, showing the inside to be marble with rows and rows of names engraved on the walls.

"Wow, it sure was a big family," Laura declared, stepping in just a little.

Stevie followed Laura into the small building. There was hardly room to turn around, but the girls stood still anyway as they got lost in reading the names. So absorbed were they in reading, they didn't hear the door closing behind them. When the iron hit the latch it made a loud clanking sound.

Laura and Stevie both screamed as they whirled around to see what was going on. "The door is shut!" Laura cried.

"Who's out there?" Stevie called through the scrolled wrought iron.

"Snacks, anyone?" Meg's voice called out, as a bag of chocolate cookies was dangled in front of the door.

"Let us out of here!" Stevie yelled.

"That's not funny, Meg," Laura said angrily.

The door swung open easily, and Molly and Meg stood laughing in front of it. "We're sorry, really," Molly said, giggling. "But how could we resist? You didn't hear us come up the path even though we called out your names."

"I guess this place is soundproof," Stevie explained. "But I did hear the part about snacks."

"Of course," Meg said sarcastically. "Here, have some," she added, holding out the bag again.

"Well, let's not eat here," Molly said. "Let's go back to the barn."

They all agreed it was a good idea, so they walked back past the stone markers and onto the path through the old rose garden. The girls were talking and laughing about the scare Meg and Molly had given the other two. Suddenly Laura's laugh turned to a scream. A look of horror spread over her face as the blood drained from her cheeks, leaving her as white as the marble statue to which she was pointing.

41

Stevie saw right away what Laura had noticed. "What the — ?" she began, walking through a bramble of dead rose bushes to reach the statue. Something was very different about this Queen of the Dead Roses. Now, in her hand the marble maiden held one rose. And it was alive!

"Okay," said Stevie, not ready to be frightened. "Which one of you two put this here on your way through?" Stevie looked accusingly at Meg and Molly.

"We didn't do it," Molly said in a shaky voice. "We got paper and pencils and the cookies, but that's it."

"We did not get a rose, Stevie!" Meg defended herself and Molly. "And besides, look at the rose. It's another one of those strange ones. The kind that weird girl gave to Laura."

Laura didn't wait to hear anymore. She turned and ran, not toward the barn but all the way to the front gate. Tears were streaming down her face. Tears of fear and tears of anger. She didn't know why, but she had a feeling that rose was put on the statue for her. When she was safely inside her own house, Laura splashed cold water on her face to wash away the feeling and the tears. She was just drying her face and hands when she heard her friends' voices downstairs.

"Laura?" Meg called out. "Are you all right?"

"I'm okay," Laura answered as she came slowly down the stairs. "I don't know what happened to me. It was just seeing that rose in the statue's hand. For some reason I got this silly idea that . . ."

"That it was for you?" Meg finished.

"Oh, I know it sounds so dumb," Laura said, throwing her long hair back over her shoulders. "My imagination was working overtime, I think."

"I'm not so sure about that," Meg said cautiously. She didn't want to upset Laura, but she did have something to tell her.

"Oh, just tell her and get it over with," Molly said to Meg. "She's going to have to find out sooner or later."

"And sooner is better so we can all start figuring out what to do about it," Stevie added.

"What are you all talking about? What do you know that I don't know? Something about the statue and the rose?" Laura anxiously looked from face to face trying to get an idea of what they were all keeping from her.

Meg held out both her hands. In one, there was a small note. In the other, there was a pile of rose petals. "I found this in your Secret Note place," Meg said. "I was just putting a note in the chimney telling you not to worry. When I reached in, there was already something there. This." She pushed her hands toward Laura.

Laura took the note, opened it, and read: *"Hi."* It was signed simply, *"Rose."*

"The Rose!" Laura said in shock. "It must be that girl! But how does she know where I live? How does she know where my hiding place is? Why is she bothering me like this?"

"Now hold on, Laura," Stevie said. "First of all we don't know it's that girl. And second of all, if it *is* her she hasn't really done anything."

"But it's like she's following us or something," Molly said, siding with Laura. "Or following Laura."

"Oh, will you all sleep over tonight?" Laura begged. "I don't want to be thinking about this all by myself all night. Please?"

Laura didn't have to say any more. All the girls agreed that a sleepover would be a great idea. It would give them the chance to keep their eyes open for clues around Laura's house. Maybe The Rose would come back and they would catch her if they watched out the window.

Mrs. Ryder agreed to the sleepover and even suggested a picnic dinner out on the back porch.

When the girls returned to Laura's house with their overnight bags, Laura already had the table set out back. The smell of fried chicken filled the air and reminded the girls of the fact that they had never had the snack Meg and Molly had brought. They ate chicken, potato salad, and Mr. Ryder's specialty, homemade biscuits. For dessert Mrs. Ryder set up bowls of ice cream toppings and let them all make their own sundaes. The fun of the picnic took Laura's mind off The Rose for a while, but when the dishes were cleared away and the girls were left alone on the old stone porch, the subject came up again.

"I never realized that your porch was a part of another house once," Stevie said, looking at the stone wall that formed the foundation.

"Yeah," said Meg. "Now that we've seen the Crispin Mansion up close I can see that these stones match the ones in the walkway that goes up to the house."

"And the path that goes around the garden," Molly added.

"And right up to that statue," Laura said quietly, feeling haunted by the memory of the rose in the marble maiden's hand.

Stevie saw the look on Laura's face and tried to make her feel better. "Hey, but isn't it so neat to have part of history right here on your own house? It's as if somehow you're connected to the Crispin family."

"Well, her house is, but she isn't," Meg corrected. "And if you *were* connected to the family, Laura, maybe you could get Stevie and me into that luncheon."

"I'd do anything to get a look inside that place," Stevie said. "It must be incredible if they left the old mansion for it."

"You'd do anything?" Meg said mischievously. "How about ballet?"

"Hey! I do have my limits!" Stevie protested. She stood up suddenly and put her hands up as if to protect herself from Meg's words. "Ballet isn't my thing."

"Just kidding," Meg laughed. "Ballet isn't the way for us to get in. But maybe we could get a job there that day helping at the luncheon. We could write a letter and sign it *'Friends 4-Ever At Your Service.'* "

"What kind of job?" Molly asked.

"You know, clearing tables or passing around the appetizers. I do that at my parents' parties." Meg was excited about her idea.

"We all do that at our parents' parties," Stevie agreed. "Sure, I could do that."

"And since it's a charity luncheon we could offer to do it for free, then she'd have to say yes!" Meg jumped up and clapped her hands together, applauding her own brilliance.

"I'll get some stationery and a pen," Laura volunteered, running into the house and back out in a flash. "Here," she said, handing Meg the paper. "Or do you want to write it, Stevie?"

"No way," Stevie said. "I don't mind passing out the Cheez Doodles at a party, but I'll leave the letter writing to Meg."

Meg smoothed the paper out on the table and wrote.

Dear Mrs. Crispin,

Stephanie Ames and I would like to offer our services to you at your charity luncheon. We are experienced appetizer passers and have passed many appetizers out at our parents' parties. We would not charge for our services and would like to help. Please call Stephanie or me (Meg) at 555-2027. Thank you for your time.

Sincerely,
Meg Milano
Friends 4-Ever At Your Service

"Great letter except for the 'Stephanie' part," Stevie said, handing the letter back to Meg.

"Stephanie sounds more formal," Meg explained. "And besides, it's no secret that Stephanie is your real name, is it?"

"Nope," said Stevie. "I guess I don't have any secrets, not from you guys, anyway."

"Me neither," said Molly.

"That can't be true," Meg argued. "But there's one way to find out. We'll play *Secrets*. You *have* to tell a secret in that game."

"Oh, do you really want to play that?" Laura asked with a strange and worried look on her face.

"Sure, let's!" said Stevie, plopping down on the floor of the porch. "Everyone get in a circle."

The other three gathered around, ready to play the game in which each person had a turn to have a secret. The others were allowed to ask two questions until someone guessed the secret. Most times the secrets were small. It was no different this time until it was Laura's turn.

Stevie's secret had to do with "borrowing" her brother Mike's soccer shin guards and leaving them at the field by mistake. Mike hadn't noticed yet, and Stevie was afraid to tell. They were gone when she went back to get them, and she was planning to buy Mike a new pair.

Meg's secret was that she was really jealous of Laura and Molly being able to go to the Crispin luncheon, but she was trying not to feel that way. Laura and Molly gave her a hug to show her they forgave her for being jealous.

Molly's secret had to do with missing her friends in Kansas sometimes. She never liked to say that out loud because she knew it made her friends at home think she would rather be in Kansas, which was not true at all.

Then it was Laura's turn. She started to speak, but before she could even get half a sentence out, tears appeared in her eyes.

"Laura! What's the matter?" Molly said, surprised to see the mood of the game change so suddenly.

"I know what the matter is," said Meg, putting an arm around Laura. "It's that rose, isn't it?"

Laura wiped the tears away. "I know I'm being so silly about it," she apologized. "Nothing has really happened, but it just makes me feel like I'm being watched or followed. I mean, she even knows my Secret Note Society hiding place!"

Meg jumped up. "We've got to get to the bottom of this mystery," she said. "Tonight we'll take turns watching out your window. If The

Rose plans to return, she'll be sorry, that's for sure!"

A happy look returned to Laura's face. She still had her fears, but she also had her friends. As the girls all spread out their sleeping bags on the tiny floor space in Laura's room, the topics of conversation went from The Rose, to the Crispin Mansion, to the Crispin luncheon, and back to The Rose. They did one potato, two potato to decide which of them would do the first watch out the window. Stevie won the decision.

"Go ahead, you guys," she said, keeping her face pressed up against the glass. "Sleep away while I sit up and guard. If I see anything I'll wake you up."

Of course none of them could sleep right away. With their pillows all close together and their sleeping bags arranged side by side, they whispered in the dark until one by one they did fall asleep.

"Good night, Stevie," Molly was the last to say. "Wake me when it's my turn."

"Uh-huh," Stevie said sleepily, her head now resting on the windowsill.

Stevie didn't see The Rose that night. In fact, no one did. Morning came and with it came stiff yawns and tired sighs from all the Friends 4-Ever.

"Well, we're a fine bunch of mystery solvers," laughed Molly.

"Uh!" Stevie said as she stretched her long legs and threw her arms up over her head. "Sorry, you guys. I guess I fell asleep before my turn was up. I'm a better soccer guard than I am a mystery guard."

"Oh, well," Laura said, clicking her retainer against the roof of her mouth. "I guess no news about The Rose is good news. To me it is, anyway."

Now Meg opened one eye as she stretched in her sleeping bag. "Wait just a minute," she said sleepily, but still with a sound of authority in her voice. "Today is the day we're going to solve this case!"

"I can't solve anything on an empty stomach," Stevie announced, holding her stomach and pretending to fall to the floor in a hunger faint.

"Me neither," agreed Molly. She twisted one of the tiny horseshoe pierced earrings she wore and looked around for her cowgirl boots and jeans.

"Oh, Molly! Please don't do that! It makes my stomach turn!" Meg covered her eyes.

"What?" Molly said innocently. "Putting on my jeans? My boots? What?"

"Twisting your pierced earring like that. Ugh!

I can't even look!" Meg still wasn't used to the idea of one of them really having pierced ears. It was one of the things that Molly had done when she was in Kansas. Meg was glad Molly was only allowed to wear studs. She was sure she'd gag if she had to see Molly's earlobes being stretched down by dangly earrings.

"Sorry," laughed Molly, giving the horseshoe one more twist just for a laugh. "Let's get dressed and eat."

"How can I eat after seeing you do that?" Meg asked. Then the smell of bacon cooking hit her in the nose and she breathed deeply. "Well, maybe I can force myself. We'll eat and then work on the case."

"Oh," said Laura. "I forgot that I have to go help my mother at the bookstore today. They just got boxes and boxes of new books in, and I said I'd help unpack."

"And I have a soccer practice today," Stevie reminded them.

"Well, Molly," Meg demanded. "And what's your excuse?"

"Riding lesson?" Molly said timidly, hating to admit that she, too, had something else to do.

"All right. All right," Meg gave in. "Then we'll just have to take today off and get back on it first thing tomorrow."

"Uh-oh," Laura groaned. "Tomorrow we can't, either. Molly and I have practice at Miss Humphrey's."

"Gosh," Molly said. "I forgot all about that. First thing tomorrow morning it's tiara time again." She rolled her eyes upward and grimaced at the thought of pinning something in her hair again.

"And right *now* it's chow time," Stevie reminded everyone. She led the way down to where Mrs. Ryder had a breakfast of eggs, bacon, and leftover biscuits all ready for them.

They had all agreed it would be better not to talk about The Rose yet in front of parents. Not until they had more facts and clues gathered. So the talk at breakfast was all about the luncheon at the Crispin Mansion and the dance program. Even Meg and Stevie could talk happily about it now that Meg had written the letter they were sure would get them in. They decided that practice or no practice the next day, they would all somehow see each other.

When the three girls left Laura's house, Laura went back upstairs to get her clipboard and paper to take to the bookstore, just in case she needed something to do if unpacking books got too boring. She stopped to look out her window and could clearly see her three friends walking home, looking tired and bedraggled. Suddenly something else caught Laura's eye. It was a shadow over near the bushes her friends were about to walk by!

From where she stood Laura could see the shadow growing bigger and bigger the closer Meg, Molly, and Stevie got to it. Fearing for their safety, Laura began banging on her window.

"Look out!" she screamed through the closed window. The shadow moved closer and closer to her friends. Laura was sure it was The Rose. "Meg!" she screamed as she pounded on the glass.

Before she could scream again, Laura watched as the shadow jumped out at the girls, causing all of them to drop their bundles and scream. Suddenly Laura was leaning against her window laughing. In a second, the girls outside were laughing, too. The huge shadow was not The Rose. It was only Stevie's eleven-year-old brother Mike and two friends of his, jumping out of the bushes to scare the Friends 4-Ever.

Still laughing as she gracefully pranced down the stairs, Laura took a minute to write a note on her unicorn stationery clipped to her clipboard.

To The Rose
The birdhouse chimney is my Secret Note
   Place
And is only for my friends and me.
Please keep your notes and roses
And just let my friends and me be!

Laura Ryder

Laura folded the note up and stuck it in her own Secret Note hiding place on her way out with her mother.

There! thought Laura. That should take care of that!

PRACTICE MAKES TROUBLE

"Quickly, girls! Quickly now!" When Miss Humphrey spoke she clapped her blue-veined hands together, causing the rows and rows of colored metal bracelets on her arms to clink and clank like a chorus line of knights in shining armor. "Faster with those costume changes, girls!" she called out to the ones backstage. "The only way to Broadway is the hard way!"

Miss Humphrey always said things like that. Sometimes the girls didn't even know what she meant. But they did know she meant business when it came to looking professional up onstage.

As Laura and Molly came hurrying onto the stage and took their places, Miss Humphrey's voice boomed out another instruction, specifically aimed at them. "You are my stars! Hold your heads up high when you come onto a stage. If the spotlight is on you look out into it. And if it isn't on you *step* into it! Stars have to look like stars!"

Laura held her head up high and looked right out into the audience.

"Bravo, Laura darling! Bravo! Now you, Molly," the teacher commanded, pushing up one of the two long scarves she wore around her head. Her eyes were shaded with heavy black eyeliner. More scarves flew out from around her waist. Her bracelets jangled. "Head high, Miss Molly! Head high!" she called out dramatically.

Molly tried to throw her head up as high as Laura's. Instead she threw her rhinestone tiara up and it hung by a hair down the side of her head. When the other girls laughed at Molly, Miss Humphrey did what she always did. She found a story to tell from her old days as a chorus girl on Broadway in New York City.

Taking a pointed-toed giant step forward, Miss Humphrey raised her index finger into the air and brought it in a hushing motion to her lips. Without saying, "Sshhhh," she had the girls' attention.

"Thank you," she said with a bow from the waist. Next she raised up both hands and began her story. "Laugh you may, girls, but when I was onstage living out of a trunk and no more, a similar thing happened. Listen and learn from what I say." She cleared her throat, gracefully put one of the waist scarves over her arm, and began.

"There was a girl in the chorus of a new show on Broadway whose name was Greta. In fact, people thought we were quite the pair since I was called Hedda, and wherever we went they said, 'There go Hedda and Greta!' Well, as I was saying, Greta also wore a crown, like yours, Molly. On opening night when the curtain was raised, Greta began her dance and her crown immediately slipped down the side of her head. She pushed it back up, but of course down it fell again. But Greta — and here's the lesson, girls — went on as though the falling crown was all a part of the performance. The audience laughed and laughed, but Greta never lost her control until after the show was over."

"Then what happened?" Molly asked.

"Then she cried her eyes out and swore she'd never appear in public again," Miss Humphrey said matter-of-factly.

"And?" Laura asked.

"And then the newspaper review came out the next morning with a headline that read, 'New Show Is A Hit! Chorus Girl Adds the Crowning Touch!' The critics loved Greta, and from that day on, the director kept the falling crown in the show. Greta, of course, went on to become Broadway's leading funny lady." The teacher threw her head back, signaling the end of the story but added one more thing. "So, my girls," she said wisely. "If we are struck by misfortune, the trick is to carry on as though what has happened was meant to be. Turn lemons into lemonade, girls. Lemons into lemonade!"

"What is this, a cooking class or ballet class?" Stevie whispered to Meg as the two of them tiptoed into the studio just in time to hear Miss Humphrey's last words of advice.

"Sssshhh!" Meg silenced Stevie. "We don't want Miss Humphrey to throw us out, do we?"

As though on cue, Miss Humphrey turned to the two newcomers and called out, "Wonderful! Welcome to our rehearsal, girls. Every show needs an audience. Every audience needs a show! This is splendid!"

For the next two hours, Stevie and Meg sat almost quietly and watched Miss Humphrey nearly as much as they watched the dancers.

"What color do you think her hair is under all those scarves?" Stevie whispered to Meg.

"No one's ever seen it," Meg replied. "In fact, that's been the greatest mystery in Camden ever since she got here from New York."

"Mystery?" Stevie said, her eyes lighting up. "Call in the Clue Club!" She giggled at her own idea.

"Right," said Meg sarcastically.

"Well, aren't you curious?" Stevie continued.

"Me and the rest of the world," Meg said, ready to drop the subject now as Miss Humphrey floated in a flurry of scarves closer to where they sat.

"Back row?" the teacher boomed. "Heads held high, remember? You're not back there to hide. You're back there to shine! Smile! Heads up! If you want to *be* something you've got to *be* seen!"

As Miss Humphrey drifted forward toward the stage again, Stevie was about to stand up and do an imitation of her. But before she had even twirled around once both she and Meg started giggling softly. Meg got up to twirl with Stevie and as she got halfway turned around, she stopped suddenly and pointed to the window. "Look!" she gasped.

Stevie stopped twirling and held onto a chair until the room stopped twirling, too. She followed Meg's finger to where it was pointing. Then she saw what Meg saw. "I don't believe it!" Stevie said, her mouth hanging open at the end of her sentence.

From where she stood on stage, Laura had been trying not to pay attention to the giggling and whispering and twirling her friends in the back were doing. But now she couldn't help but notice that both of them stood motionless, staring open-mouthed at the window across the room. She turned her crowned head in the direction of the window, and a look of shock spread over her face.

Laura stood as still as the statue in the garden at the Crispin Mansion. Immediately she recognized the face at the window. "It's her!" she called out in the middle of the rehearsal. It was the girl from the Yellow Brick Road restaurant. The same girl with the marble-white face and glasses and the stick-straight hair pulled back with a rose-colored bow stood looking in at Laura.

"Laura!" shouted Miss Humphrey a little sternly. "We must look *over* the audience, not *into* it. That way we won't be distracted from our performance!"

"But Miss Humph — " Laura began.

"The show must go on, my dear! The show must go on! Continue please, Laura!" Miss Humphrey swept down an aisle and stood directly in front of where Laura was on the stage. Now Laura had no choice but to continue her dancing.

"It's okay," whispered Molly, who had also seen the strange girl's face peering in at Laura. "Stevie and Meg are going after her."

Laura looked out into the audience just in time to see her two friends running out the door. Without missing a step in her performance, Laura managed to look toward the window and see Stevie's long hair flying out behind her. Meg followed, and soon the two were out of Laura's sight.

"Well?" whispered Molly through a smile. She still looked straight ahead with her head held high.

"I don't know," Laura answered through her

own smile. She did the next few movements, which brought her behind Molly. "I just saw them running, but I didn't see the girl anymore." She moved gracefully across the stage and twirled back to Molly's side.

"What's taking them so long?" Molly asked without moving her lips even a little. She did a sweeping bend to the floor and came up for Laura's answer.

"Oh, I hope they're all right," Laura worried as her arms formed a perfect circle over her head and she swayed back and forth with the rest of the line of dancers.

"Reach, Laura dear!" Miss Humphrey called out. "For the stars, girls!"

Laura reached higher just as Stevie and Meg reappeared in the doorway of the dance studio. She could see that they were out of breath as they leaned their backs against the doorjamb, gulping air and holding their stomachs.

"Wonderful job, girls!" Miss Humphrey said, concluding the rehearsal at last. She waved her scarves through the air, applauding her students and making her bracelets clink noisily again.

Costumed dancers flew off the stage like birds heading south for the winter. Laura and Molly shed their dance clothes and hurried to join Stevie and Meg out front.

"What happened?" Laura asked excitedly.

"Did you get her?" Molly added.

"Where is she now?" Laura breathed as she played nervously with the strings of a pink-and-blue friendship bracelet on her left wrist.

"Hold it," Stevie said, still clutching her stomach and trying to catch her breath. "We ran out to catch her, but before we even got out there we lost her."

"Yeah," Meg added, struggling to catch her breath, too. "She sure has her disappearing act down. Now we see her, now we don't."

"And now we wish we never did!" Laura said with that frightened look on her face again.

As Laura and Molly gathered up their ballet things, Meg and Stevie talked about their first reaction to seeing that face in the window.

"I swear, I thought I was dreaming!" Stevie said.

"I thought I was having a nightmare!" Meg said, topping Stevie.

"But her face isn't really scary," Molly defended the strange girl. "Why do I feel sorry for her?"

"I don't know, Molly. I feel sorry for *me*." Laura tucked her leg warmers into her purple ballet bag. "You know, I feel like I'm being haunted or something."

"But she's real," Stevie said.

"Then how does she manage to disappear into thin air all the time?" Laura argued. "And how does she manage to just appear? And how did she get in the garden to put the rose in the statue's hand? And the notes in my hiding place?"

"Sorry, Laura," Meg said. "We don't know some of those things for sure. We didn't actually see that girl put the rose in the statue's hand. And we don't know if it really was her who put the notes in your chimney."

On the way home, the four girls tried and tried to figure out something, anything about the face at the window. As they were walking, they started hearing footsteps and whispering behind them. Stevie whirled around quickly and caught the culprits.

"You guys!" she sputtered, pushing up her baseball cap and settling her hands on her hips. "Mike, can't you find something better to do than to bother us?"

It was Stevie's brother and two of his friends,

Willy and Simon. Whenever they weren't playing basketball, soccer, baseball, or street hockey,
they played "pain in the neck."

"The game they really excel at!" Stevie always
said.

"What's the matter?" Mike teased. "Can't the
Super Snoops take a joke?"

"A funny one, yeah," was Stevie's answer.

Willy tugged a handful of Stevie's hair as he
ran around in front of the four girls. Mike followed, giving Laura's long locks a good yank,
and Simon took care of the other two girls, taking
a handful of hair in each hand.

"We're outta here!" yelled Willy.

"Nice talking to you," Mike laughed as he ran
away.

"Be seein' ya," Simon called out.

"In your dreams," Stevie muttered under her
breath as she tried to smooth her rumpled
hair.

"Well, there go a bunch of good-for-nothings!"
said Molly, fixing her own hair.

"You can say that again," Stevie agreed.

"Well, there go a bunch of good-for-nothings!"
Molly repeated, making everyone laugh.

"Actually they were good for something,"
Laura said thoughtfully. "They were good for
changing the subject."

"And speaking of 'the subject,' " Meg said, bringing "the subject" back, "we're meeting at the barn tomorrow at noon. Can you all be there?"

Three heads bobbed up and down, and Stevie spoke for all of them when she said, "We wouldn't miss it for the world."

"Or even for The Rose," added Laura quietly.

TOO MANY MYSTERIES

Two girls dressed in purple shorts, purple T-shirts, and hot pink scrunchy socks walked through the big iron gates of the Crispin Mansion. Except for the fact that one girl had long brown hair and the other girl had short brown hair, the two looked almost identical from the back. Up close, though, it was easy to see that Laura and Molly had just decided to make this day "Twins Day." Everything they wore had to be the same, except for Molly's pierced earrings, of course.

"But you have your retainer," Molly said, defending her difference when Laura pointed it out. "So we're both wearing extra metal."

Laura laughed at Molly's logic. The "twins" linked arms as they skipped through the gates and up the path toward the big mansion. The bright sun and warm breeze should have given the place a bright and happy feeling. But even with sun lighting every nook and cranny of the house and gardens, the girls in purple still felt a little nervous once they were inside the gates. They stopped skipping when they got to the barn.

"No Stevie and Meg," Molly said, looking all around as she spoke.

"Then we can't go in," Laura reminded Molly. Their rule was that they would only go into the barn together. Otherwise it seemed just too spooky.

"Well, then let's explore some more. We can look in some of the windows we haven't looked in yet." Molly turned to go toward the house.

"Wait up," said Laura, hurrying to catch up. "Don't leave me alone."

"I wouldn't," Molly assured her.

"I don't know how Nancy Drew does it," Laura said. "That girl is never afraid of anything."

"That girl is also just a character in a book.

And all her cases are just made up. Our mystery is real and so are we," Molly explained.

"And so are my jitters!" Laura said, knocking her knees together in an exaggerated state of fear.

First the two girls peeked into the kitchen window. They saw a huge room with white tile counters and glass-doored cabinets. The cabinets were empty except for some old cracked plates, a pitcher, and a flower vase with painted roses on the side.

"Roses again," Laura said when she spotted the vase.

"Well, it is a popular flower," Molly laughed. "You can't be thinking every rose there ever was has something to do with *our* Rose."

Laura laughed at herself. "You're right. I'm being silly, I know." She left the kitchen window and moved along the side of the house to a fringed velvet curtained window. It was clear that this room was the library. From floor to ceiling shelves of books lined all four walls. Laura tried to read some of the titles of books that were closest to the window.

"*Famous English Gardens* by Sir Alfred Cedrick," she read out to Molly. "And *Experts' Guide to Gardening*," Laura called out. "Hey, it looks like this whole bookcase is full of books about gardening."

"Maybe even the whole book collection," Molly added, seeing some other titles on another shelf. "Listen to these: *All the Pretty Flowers, Where the Wildflowers Are, Roses Most Rare, Bouquets and —* " Molly didn't have a chance to finish.

"Wait!" Laura stopped her. "Go back one."

"*Bouquets and —* " Molly repeated.

"No, before that," Laura said excitedly.

"*Roses Most Rare,*" read Molly. "Oh! Roses again!"

"But isn't that so weird that there would be all these books on flowers here?" Laura went on. "Not weird, but coincidental or something."

"Or interesting, anyway," Molly said, moving around to the bedroom window with the roses etched onto the glass. She peeked in. Everything looked the same as it did the first day they were there. At first glance it did, anyway.

Laura moved in next to Molly and looked in, too. Suddenly she shouted out, "Molly! Look!"

"What? I *am* looking," Molly said, pressing her face even closer to the glass. "Oh! The dress!" she said, suddenly seeing what Laura saw.

As both girls looked closer and harder they could see that the closet door was opened more than it had been that first day. And lying on the bare mattress of the canopy bed was a filmy, rose-colored gown spread out as if someone had planned to wear it soon.

"Now I know *that* dress was not on *that* bed before," Laura said with certainty. "Somebody has been in this house!"

"But how would they get in? We checked all the doors before. Well, Stevie did, anyway," said Molly.

"Did what?" Stevie's voice said, coming up behind them. Laura and Molly jumped and let out a startled scream.

"Hey, sorry!" Stevie apologized. "Is my face *that* bad? I wasn't trying to scare you guys. Meg and I went to the barn first."

"And when we didn't see you we figured you might be over here poking around," Meg finished.

"You were right," Molly said. "And our poking around paid off. Take a look in this window!"

Stevie and Meg looked in the window. "What?" asked Stevie.

"The dress!" Meg said. "See the dress on the

bed? And the closet door is opened more! This is getting too spooky for me!"

"Me, too," Laura agreed.

"And now we have another mystery to add to our list," said Molly as she moved closer to Laura.

"Don't you think someone had to be in here?" Laura said again.

"I checked all the doors before," said Stevie, "but I didn't check the windows. And upstairs there's another door from that balcony." Stevie pointed to a white railing that went around an upstairs porch.

"Upstairs is impossible to get to," Meg started to say. But before she could say any more, Stevie was already doing her tree-climbing swing up a column that supported the porch.

"Stevie!" Laura shouted.

"Relax, gang," Stevie said calmly as she shinnied up the column and swung one leg over the white railing. "I'm already up."

"What can you see in the windows?" Molly asked curiously as Stevie cupped her hands over her eyes and peered in one room.

"Nothing. Empty. Just dust." Stevie moved over to another window. "Same story in this room," she called down to the girls. "Empty."

"Try the door," Meg shouted up.

Stevie rattled the doorknob. It turned in her hand but nothing happened. "Locked up tight," she told Meg. "There's no way anyone could have gotten in from here. And besides, the floors are so dusty there would be footprints."

"Come down now, Stevie," Laura pleaded. She huddled close to Molly.

"Hey," Stevie laughed. "From up here you two look like a bunch of grapes!"

Meg looked at Laura and Molly dressed in purple and clinging tightly to each other. Then she laughed, too. "Well, speaking of grapes," she said, "I brought some for the club snack." She held up her bulging blue tote bag, which she'd gotten at the aquarium a long time ago.

"Then let's go eat them," Stevie said as she slid down the column and landed perfectly balanced on both blue-sneakered feet.

Meg led the way back over to the barn. Together she and Stevie pulled the big door open just enough for all four of them to slip inside single file. Once inside, Meg closed the barn door behind them and followed the streak of sunlight that led upstairs to the hayloft. The others followed close behind, holding onto each others' shirts and arms for a feeling of safety.

"Grapes for the group!" Meg called out as she reached the top step and started to dump the tote bag out on the hay table.

"Wait a minute!" Laura said the second she stepped up into the hayloft. "Don't you notice something different?"

"What? Everything looks neat and tidy," Stevie said. "That's different for *my* room but not so different for our club meeting place."

"Except that we didn't leave the place all neat and tidy, remember?" Meg said, now that she saw what Laura meant. "Remember? We found the rose in the statue's hand and didn't come back here."

The girls agreed that something was very different about their meeting place. All their things had been rearranged. Fixed up. Cleaned up.

"I don't like this one bit," Laura said.

"But the point is what are we going to do about it?" Meg said. "If someone has been up here, then who was it?"

"Maybe it was your brother and the two pains in the neck," Molly suggested. "They've been bugging us since the beginning of time. Maybe they came up here and moved all our stuff."

"Impossible," Stevie said. "In a million years they'd never come up here and clean up. If you saw Mike's room you'd know right away that the words *clean*, *neat*, and *tidy* aren't even in his vocabulary."

"And everyone knows Willy's a slob," Molly added.

"No, it couldn't have been them. And besides, I don't think they even know we come here," Meg pointed out.

"Well, I know I didn't tell them," said Stevie. "Why would I?"

Meg tapped her knuckles against a splintery roof rafter as she called the meeting to order. "The Friends 4-Ever Clue Club meeting is now officially called to order."

"Yeah," commented Stevie, looking around at all the club pencils lined up, the hay bale chairs straightened, and the boxes of club stationery piled neatly on the hay bale table. "I'd call this a little *too* orderly."

Meg ignored the interruption. "Here's what we have to do," she said, sounding quite sure of her plan. "It started out that we just had one mystery to solve: finding the girl from the Yellow Brick Road. But now we have a lot of mysteries to solve. The only way we're going to be able to do it is if we split up."

"Split up!" Laura said, horrified at the thought

of having to track down clues alone.

Meg understood. "Well, how about we just split up into pairs? Laura, you and Molly go together, and Stevie and I will."

"Go where?" asked Laura.

"Why don't Stevie and I investigate the barn and house mysteries, while you two work on trying to find out who the girl with the glasses is?" Meg looked around at the other club members to see if they liked her plan.

"Great idea!" Molly said, jumping up and ready to go.

"Well, as long as there are two of us I guess it'll be all right," Laura said hesitantly.

"It sounds absotively posolutely stupendous!" Stevie cheered. "Once again Meg Milano leads the Friends 4-Ever on the path to greatness."

"Or to trouble," Laura said worriedly. She threw her long hair over to one side and peeked out of the strands that fell over one eye.

"Don't worry about a thing, Laura," Molly said. "Once we find that girl we'll just ask her why she gave you the rose in the first place. There's probably a perfectly logical explanation."

"Yeah, like she wanted to poison me with that thorn, remember?" Laura said.

"Forget about the thorn," Meg instructed.

"Right now all we have to think about is tracking down some of these clues. Stevie, the first place you and I are going is to the library."

"The library?" Stevie said with surprise. "We won't have time to read if we expect to solve this mystery."

"If we expect to solve this mystery," Meg explained, "I think we'll *have* to read. I have a feeling that if we could just find out more about the house we'll understand the clues better."

"You might be right, Meg," said Molly. "And that gives me the idea that if we knew more about the roses we'd be closer to solving that mystery."

"That's it, then," Meg said in her official-sounding voice. "Stevie and I will go to the library, and you and Laura will take those two roses and the rose petals and try to find out whose garden they came from."

"You're a genius, Meg," Laura said, feeling proud of her friend's ability to organize everything so quickly. "I don't know how you think so fast."

"Elementary, my dear Laura. Elementary," sniffed Meg in her best British accent. "Have a grape, my dears!" Meg passed the bunch of grapes around, and each of the Clue Club sleuths popped a couple into their mouths as they marched out the barn door.

Before they left the grounds of the Crispin estate the girls formed a small circle. Each one stuck out her right hand into the middle of the circle. Hands piled on hands, they once again made their solemn promise to each other.

"Friends 4-Ever," four voices said together. Then two by two they went their separate ways, agreeing to meet later at Meg's house.

While Laura and Molly tried to track down the garden from which the unusually-colored roses had come, Meg and Stevie spent their time stalking the stacks of books on the history of Camden at the library.

"I think we need to talk to Mrs. Kelly, the librarian," Meg told Stevie as she put away the last history book left to look at. "There must be something somewhere about the old Crispin Mansion."

The librarian gladly checked the computer listings for the girls. Squinting her eyes as she tried to read the small print on the screen, she shook her head as the titles moved by. "Nothing. Nothing. Nothing. Aha!" she finally said. "There is one book written by a man named Wallace Pearce. Now that I see this I remember the book. It's the only copy around, and the listing here shows that it's over at the Historical Society library now. But I can have it brought here tomorrow if you can wait."

"We'll take it!" Stevie said, anxious to get out of the library and onto a soccer field, or bike path, or anywhere books weren't.

"Yes," said Mrs. Kelly, "I think this is what you're looking for. It has the history of the Crispin family and a whole section on the Crispin Mansion itself."

The girls filled out a book reserve form and thanked the helpful woman. Then they ran to meet Laura and Molly at Meg's house.

"How'd you guys make out?" Stevie asked when they arrived and found the purple-dressed pair waiting on Meg's front step.

Molly was already up and on her feet, ready to report on their findings. "At first," she said, "we walked up and down every street in Crispin Landing. We checked in every garden, front yards and back, but we didn't find any roses that matched The Rose roses."

"But then," Laura added excitedly, "Molly had the brilliant idea to take the roses to Mr.

Dimitri's flower shop and ask him about them!"

"Brilliant!" agreed Meg.

"So that's exactly what we did," Molly continued, "and Mr. Dimitri told us plenty."

"He said first of all he doesn't sell this kind of rose because it's a very rare kind and only grows in hothouses," Laura explained.

"My house is hot," Stevie joked.

"He meant greenhouses," Molly explained unnecessarily.

"Duh," Stevie said, hanging her mouth half open and putting one finger on her bottom lip.

"Well, he also said that the first rose is exactly like the rose from the statue, which is exactly like the rose petals that were in my Secret Note hiding place," Laura continued.

"So in other words you had about as much luck as we did," said Stevie. "All we got was a book that we can't even get until tomorrow."

"Hey," Meg defended their efforts, "we know more than we did this morning, right? And tomorrow we'll continue our investigations."

"Can't," Laura said.

"Can't," said Molly, too.

"Another rehearsal?" Stevie gasped. "Drill, drill, drill. What is Miss Humphrey running, a ballet army or something? There can't be anything you don't already know."

"Tomorrow is special. Mrs. Crispin is coming to watch. She wants to see the performance before the luncheon, and she's going to explain where we come in and go out and all that."

"And while we're on the subject of going in and out of her house, that reminds me. We still haven't heard back after our letter to Mrs. Crispin," Meg said thoughtfully.

"Maybe we'll just have to show up at the rehearsal tomorrow and meet her face to face. Tell me, how could she refuse a face like this?" Stevie puckered her lips too sweetly, smiled a little smile, and fluttered her eyelashes.

"Easily!" said the other three all together.

"Then, how about a face like this?" This time Stevie stretched out both sides of her mouth with two fingers, stuck out her tongue, and turned up her eye so none of the blue showed, only white.

"Yeecch! Gross!" said Molly.

Stevie laughed as she let her face go back to its original freckled shape. "Well, I still say we should show up when she's there and ask her if she got our letter."

"It's a deal," said Meg, standing up to go into

82

her house. "We'll all meet at Miss Humphrey's studio tomorrow."

The other girls turned to go, too, and for the second time that day they said their good-byes.

Looking at her purple shirt, Molly joked, "Sorry to break up the bunch."

Laura held out her grape-colored shirt and joked back. "We had a grape day, all right."

"Yes, a vine day indeed," Molly threw back.

Stevie couldn't take any more grape jokes. She tugged on Molly's shirt sleeve and pulled her in the direction of their street, Half Moon Lane. "Time for the grape escape!" she said, unable to resist a joke of her own.

Laura had a short walk up to the corner and across to her house. " 'Bye, guys!" she called out as she did her best ballet leaps all the way to her front yard. Her last leap landed her right in front of the birdhouse where she had left the note for The Rose.

Laura reached in the chimney and felt around with her hand. Nothing. She felt around a little more and brought her hand out holding a piece of paper. Slowly she unfolded it, and then breathed a big sigh of relief. It wasn't a note from The Rose. It was a note from Meg.

Dear Laura,
   It isn't The Rose
   Who is stopping by.
   It's me, Meg Milano
   Just to say "Hi!"
   Why am I here?
   Here's a clue —
   I'm here to give
   This note to you!
      Yours 'til the window panes are cured,

Meg

THE DANCE OF THE ROSE

"Hurry up, Laura!" Mrs. Ryder yelled up from downstairs. "You'll be late to your rehearsal."

From inside her closet Laura's voice, muffled by the clothes hanging there, called back, "I can't find my ballet bag!"

"Look in your closet," shouted her mother.

"I am! But it's not here." Laura was starting to get frustrated. She'd spent the last twenty minutes searching everywhere in her room for the purple bag that held all the things she needed for rehearsal. In a room as small as Laura's, twenty minutes of searching meant looking in the same places over and over again.

This was her third search of the closet.

Suddenly she remembered where the bag probably was. On the hook in the dressing room at Miss Humphrey's studio. She must have left it there after her lesson the other day. With all the mysteries that were so far unsolved, Laura felt happy to have at least solved this one.

"Coming, Laura?" Mrs. Ryder called up one last time.

"Coming," Laura answered as she floated down the stairs empty-handed.

"What, no luck?" her mother asked.

Laura explained everything to her mother as they got into the car. Mrs. Ryder was going to drop Molly and Laura off at Miss Humphrey's on her way to the bookstore.

"At least I hope it's there." Laura finished her explanation just as the car pulled up in front of Molly's house.

"Hi, Mrs. Ryder. Hi, Laura," Molly said cheerfully as she opened the back door and threw her own ballet bag onto the seat. "Where's your bag?"

Laura went through her whole story again for Molly and by the time she was finished saying, "At least I hope it's there," *they* were there. Both girls jumped out, said good-bye to Laura's mother, and rushed inside.

Miss Humphrey was at the door to greet them. "Hurry, girls! Time is of the essence! If you're Broadway bound, you have to be on the train!"

"There she goes again," giggled Molly. "Broadway. Always Broadway. All I wanted was to learn a little ballet. I never even thought of leaving Camden to do it!"

Laura laughed as she and Molly pushed through the beaded curtain that blocked the doorway to the dressing room. It was noisy, as usual, as all the other girls were hurrying to get their costumes on. Everyone was especially excited because Mrs. Crispin was going to be there to watch. Laura was relieved to see her bag hanging just where she'd hoped it would be. She and Molly exchanged greetings with the others and started pulling their own things out of their bags.

Laura pulled out her tights, her ballet shoes, and then rummaged around trying to find the tiara. Thinking she was pulling out the satin cape, Laura suddenly gasped. "Molly! Look!"

In fact, all the girls turned to see what Laura was calling attention to. What they saw was Laura holding up a lovely, rose-colored gown. It was not her regular costume.

"It's beautiful!" said Cindy, one of the other girls in the class.

"Where did you get it?" asked Hilary, another dancer.

"Laura!" Molly whispered, breathlessly. "It's the gown from the house! The one from the bed! How did you get it?"

"I didn't," Laura said in a frightened voice. "It got me!"

Just then Miss Humphrey came sailing through the beaded curtain shouting, "Costumes! Costumes, girls! Mrs. Crispin will be here momentarily! Lilies," she said, turning to the group dressed in white, "straighten your leaves. Daffodils, turn those yellow collars up." Miss Humphrey went from girl to girl, checking to be sure everyone looked just right. Then she came to Laura, who still stood holding the rose-colored gown in one hand. In her other hand she held a note. It read: *A one-of-a-kind dress for a one-of-a-kind girl.*

"That's perfect, Laura dear!" Miss Humphrey exclaimed as she saw the beautiful gown. "In the future you must ask if you wish to change your costume, but in this case I can see that your performance will benefit from the change. It's a lovely dress! Was it your grandmother's?"

"Ah, no," Laura started to explain that she had no idea whose it was or why it was in her bag.

"Put it on, dear. Put it on," Miss Humphrey hurried her. Just then she heard a woman's voice calling out her name from somewhere on the other side of the beaded curtain.

"Girls! Mrs. Crispin is here! Are you ready to put your best foot forward?" The teacher looked over her group of performers. "Lovely," she said. "Each and every one of you. And Laura, your *Dance of the Rose* will be sensational in that gown. Now, good luck to all of you," she said as she blew kisses to the air and swept back out through the beads.

As the other girls lined up, straightening their leaves, turning up their collars, and pulling out their petals, Molly stood open-mouthed, looking at Laura. "You look so, so beautiful, Laura," she said, thinking she'd never before seen her friend look quite so striking. "That dress fits you perfectly. It's as if it was made for you."

Laura looked at herself in the mirrored wall opposite the hooks and cubbies. Even she could not believe the reflection that looked back at her. Although she was never one to brag or act conceited, one word slipped out of her mouth. "Beautiful," she whispered. Then she realized how it might sound. "The dress, I mean. It is the most beautiful dress I've ever seen."

"Looking through the window, and seeing it

just lying on the bed, I couldn't tell that it was *this* pretty," Molly said, walking around Laura to get a view of the flowing skirt and puffed sleeves. "But isn't this so weird? And who wrote the note?"

"I'm sure I know," Laura said. "I've seen that handwriting before. On the note that was in my birdhouse chimney."

"The Rose?" Molly said in surprise. "You think so? Oh, Laura, this is too, too creepy. Take it off right now."

Before Laura had a chance to do anything, strains of the opening music reached through the beaded curtain and into their ears.

"It's starting!" Laura whispered. "I can't now." The music swelled, and the Lilies and Daffodils drifted gracefully onto the stage. Molly, in her rainbow-colored costume, was next. And following all of the others was Laura, the star of *The Dance of the Rose*. The main spotlight caught her the second her pointed toe found its mark on the center of the stage. And even over the singing of the violins, Laura was able to hear three distinct gasps from the darkened audience section.

"The dress!" Laura heard Meg's voice exclaim in a loud whisper.

"What the . . . ?" she heard Stevie's voice out there in the dark.

"That gown!" another, unfamiliar voice said aloud.

The show must go on, Laura heard Miss Humphrey's voice saying in her mind. She knew that dress or no dress, she had to keep her head held high and her eyes above the audience. The music carried her across the stage while the Lilies and Daffodils did their best to shine from the background.

Laura and Molly exchanged looks, but tried to concentrate on their special scene together when the Rainbow and the Rose dance their duet center stage. This time they didn't talk through smiling teeth as they danced. They knew that their performance had to be perfect for Mrs. Crispin.

"If you want to talk," Miss Humphrey always said to the talkers during class, "find a career in radio, not in ballet!"

Laura wasn't thinking about a career in anything right now. All she was thinking about was getting through the performance and getting out of the rose-colored gown. Even though the dress moved easily with every motion, every step, and even though it made her look more like the star she was supposed to be, the gown made Laura feel trapped in a cage of chiffon.

Meg noticed the strange look on Laura's face. Usually Laura looked completely comfortable and at home on stage. But something was definitely different this time.

"I hope she's all right," Meg whispered to Stevie.

"What I want to know is where she got the dress," Stevie said, still trying to figure it all out.

"Maybe it isn't the same one," Meg reasoned. "Maybe it just looks like the other one."

"There couldn't be two dresses like that one," Stevie argued. "They don't even make dresses like that anymore."

"I love how you say that, like you know something about dresses." Meg laughed quietly. "Do you even own a dress?"

"You know what I mean," Stevie said to defend herself.

"Sshhh!" came a hushing from somewhere else.

Both girls looked at each other and mouthed the same words. "Miss Humphrey." They remained quiet for the rest of the performance, but couldn't help but nudge each other and point to Mrs. Crispin and the small group of women with her.

"Mrs. Crispin," Meg silently formed the words with her lips.

"I know," Stevie returned without sound. She looked over at the profile of Mrs. Crispin who sat straight and tall in her chair, watching only Laura. Even in the dark, Stevie could see Mrs. Crispin's thick, snow-white hair pulled back into a neat bun with a navy-blue bow pinned above it. Her navy and white dress was perfectly pressed, and the single string of pearls she wore hung right to the second button. Even in the dark, Stevie could see that Mrs. Crispin was what her mother would have called "a lovely woman."

Just as Meg was about to form the words, "Isn't she beautiful?" the music stopped, the lights went on, and Mrs. Crispin and the other women began applauding.

On stage, Laura and Molly stepped forward to take their final bow while the Lilies and Daffodils waited and then stepped forward to join the two stars. Next, Miss Humphrey walked out onto the stage as her dancers stopped bowing and began applauding for her.

"Thank you," said Miss Humphrey, her armload of bangle bracelets jingling and her scarves following her onto the stage. "Now today, we are honored to have as our guests Mrs. Crispin and the charity luncheon committee. And Mrs. Crispin would like to take this opportunity to tell us the details of the luncheon and our part in it."

As the Lilies, Daffodils, Rainbow, and Rose stood politely still, Mrs. Crispin stood and spoke to them. She complimented them all on their fine performance and explained what time they should arrive at her house and where they should enter on the day of the big event. She said she was happy to meet all of them and looked forward to seeing them again at the luncheon.

"Thank you, Mrs. Crispin," Miss Humphrey said, taking back the stage. She turned to the dancers and said, "Girls, you may be excused now. Take your costumes home with you today so they may be cleaned and pressed before the performance. Move along now, quickly and quietly. Your exit from the stage should always be made as gracefully as your entrance onto it."

The girls left the stage as Miss Humphrey instructed them to, but before Laura had a chance to slip behind the curtain, Mrs. Crispin stopped her.

"My dear," she said sweetly.

Laura turned and looked up into the clear blue

eyes that had been watching her so closely for the last hour. "Yes, Mrs. Crispin?" she answered.

"That gown," the stately woman began, "may I ask where you got it?"

A look of concern came over Laura's face as she answered. "Well, uh, I'm not really sure. You see, it was just in my bag when I got here this morning, and I don't know how it got there." Laura started nervously over-explaining what she herself didn't even understand. "I mean, the first time I saw it was through the window with the roses on it. It was in the closet, then it was on the bed, and before I knew it, there it was in my bag. I don't even have any idea whose it is or where it came from or why I have it. All I know is I'm going to take it off and never put it on again!" She was close to tears as she poured out her story to the white-haired woman.

"Dear, dear," Mrs. Crispin said kindly. "I think I may know some of the answers for you."

"You do?" Laura asked, looking through the puddles that covered her fast-blinking eyes. "But I don't understand."

Mrs. Crispin began to explain, and Stevie, Meg, and Molly moved in beside Laura in time

95

to hear. "The gown you're wearing was mine when I was a young girl, probably just your age. I'm sure I don't know how it got into your bag, but I do hope you will wear it again. It looks so lovely on you and reminds me of a very beautiful time in my life. I used to dance, too."

"You did?" Stevie blurted out in disbelief. It was hard for her to imagine this reserved woman ever floating across a stage in the rose-colored gown. She corrected herself. "I mean, oh, that must have really been a long time ago!"

Mrs. Crispin laughed as Stevie realized that her second remark was even worse than her first one. "No," said Stevie, as her face blushed enough to make all the freckles blend in. "I mean, I bet you were really terrific!"

"Now, there." Mrs. Crispin smiled. "I'm sure that's really what you were trying to say all along." Then she threw back her head and laughed. "You're a charming little girl," she said, patting Stevie's head. "What is your name, dear?"

Meg answered for her. "Stephanie Ames. And I'm Meg Milano."

"Ah yes!" Mrs. Crispin said. "I've heard those names before, haven't I?"

"We sent you a letter asking if we could pass

out stuff at your luncheon," Stevie explained. "But really my name is Stevie. I mean, that's what my friends call me."

"May I call you Stevie?" Mrs. Crispin asked.

"Call me anything but late for dinner," Stevie flipped back. "No, just kidding, Mrs. Crispin," she added politely. "Yes, please call me Stevie."

Mrs. Crispin was laughing again. "My," she said, "I haven't laughed so hard in I don't know how long. And tell me, are you all friends?"

Molly answered this time. "Friends 4-Ever!" Then she went on to tell Mrs. Crispin all about the great friendship they'd had practically since the day they were born. "And except for when I moved to Kansas, we've never been separated."

"Well, then, I certainly wouldn't want you to be separated on the day of the luncheon," Mrs. Crispin said with a twinkle in her eye. "It won't be necessary for you and Meg to, as you say 'pass out stuff,' but I believe I do have something for you to do that day."

"You do?" Meg asked curiously. "Anything! What is it?"

"Well, why don't we just save it for the day of the luncheon. Would that be agreeable to you girls?" Their new acquaintance picked up her navy purse, reached out her hand, and rested it on Laura's shoulder. "You will wear the gown, won't you, dear?"

Mrs. Crispin was such a nice woman, thought Laura to herself. How could Laura say no? "Of course I'll wear it, Mrs. Crispin," Laura replied softly.

"Thank you, dear," the woman said sincerely.

"No," Meg said. "Thank *you*."

"Yeah, really," Stevie added. "You're making our dream come true."

Mrs. Crispin turned to Laura, smiled, and said, "And you're making a little dream of mine come true, too."

THE SECRET IN
THE OLD BOOK

"Gosh," Laura said to her three friends on their way home from the ballet rehearsal. "You don't think she thinks *I* took the dress or anything, do you?"

"Why in the world would she think that?" Meg asked.

"Well, she didn't even ask about the window with the roses on it or the closet or the bed. I mentioned all those things without really saying they were at *her* old house." Laura fidgeted uncomfortably.

"Old mansion," Stevie corrected.

"Maybe she was so interested in the gown that she didn't really think about where you got it," Molly suggested. "You noticed how she was just watching you the whole time, didn't you?"

"You're probably right," Laura agreed. "But when we see her again, I want to tell her that we've been over at her old hou — mansion, I mean."

"She won't care, I bet," Stevie said. "If she used to dance, she probably used to explore, and have clubs, and do all the same things we do."

"Wouldn't that be funny if she used to have meetings in the barn, too?" Molly laughed.

"Well, maybe *she* didn't," Meg said. "But her kids might have. I don't know how long that house has been there, even." Then she remembered the library. "Hey, today's the day the book we want is going to be at the library!"

Even Stevie was anxious to go back there this time. "The clue we need *must* be in that old book," she said. "Why don't we all go look at it right now?"

"First we have to drop off our ballet things," Laura said. "I'm not taking any chances by leaving my bag around this time. And besides, if this gown can suddenly appear, it might suddenly disappear just as easily."

"I don't think it's going to do that, Laura," Meg said thoughtfully. "I think in your bag is exactly where someone wants it to stay."

"Oooo, Meg," squealed Laura. "Don't say things like that! It makes me have the shivers. Look at my arms!" She stuck out both arms to show that the hairs were standing up. Her ballet bag fell down off her shoulder, and Stevie caught it for her before it hit the ground. A bit of the rose-colored gown spilled over the top of the bag.

"Hey," said Stevie, stuffing the gown back in. "Maybe *someone* wants the gown to stay in the bag, but it looks like the gown has ideas of its own!" Stevie stuck both hands out in the direction of the bag that was back on Laura's shoulder. "Back! Back, you galloping gown, you!" she ordered.

The laughter lasted all the way to Laura's house where she and Molly both stuck their bags right inside the front door.

"Next stop, the Crispin Landing Library!" Meg announced, leading the way up Crispin Landing to the main street where the library was.

As soon as they walked inside the door of the red brick building the girls automatically started *sshhhing* each other.

"Sshhh!" Laura said when Molly cleared her throat.

"Sshhh!" Meg said when Laura *sshhhed* Molly.

"Sshhh!" both Stevie and Molly said to the other two *sshhhers*.

Then all of them covered their mouths trying to hold in the giggles.

"Good afternoon, girls!" said Mrs. Kelly, the librarian, in a normal voice. "I see you've come for your book."

The girls looked around to see who else might be sitting at the study tables in the middle of the room. No one. Stevie peeked around the shelves of books to see if anyone was in any of the aisles. No one.

"It's all right," the librarian reassured them. "We're empty today. Everyone must be out enjoying the good weather. But step over here and I'll show you the book you wanted."

"This could be the moment of truth," said Meg dramatically.

"It also could be the moment of mental misery," Stevie moaned. "Look at the size of that book! It's gonna take all four of us just to lift it off the counter and move it to a table."

"We can use the book cart," Molly suggested. "Come on guys, help me lift it."

Mrs. Kelly carefully slid the big, leather-bound book across the counter to the girls. "Be gentle," she warned. "It's very old and very valuable."

Together the four friends placed the thick book carefully on the wheeled cart. Embossed in the dark green leather was the title, *The Crispins in Camden, A Family History* by Wallace Pearce. Laura and Molly picked out the closest table and settled themselves into two straight-backed wooden chairs.

"Put it right here where all of us can see it," Laura said, patting a spot in the middle of the table.

"Isn't it a beautiful book?" Meg said as she and Stevie lifted it off the cart and placed it on the spot Laura had patted. "It looks like Merlin's book of magic or something."

"Well, let's see just how magical it really is," Molly said excitedly. "If it has the answers to our mysteries then it truly is a magical book."

For the next hour and a half four heads stayed bent over the giant book reading all about the first Crispins to come to Camden and all their relatives, right up to the marriage of Helen Pearce and William Hamden Crispin III.

"Hey!" Meg said, figuring out the dates in her head. "Helen Pearce must be Mrs. Crispin!"

"Good, Meg," said Stevie sarcastically. "You can read! It says that right here in the book: *'Helen Pearce married William Hamden Crispin III.'* "

"But what I mean is that she is *our* Mrs. Crispin, and the author, Wallace Pearce, must be her younger brother." Meg explained.

"She's right," Laura agreed, doing some date figuring herself. "And it also says here that Helen and William moved into the old Crispin Mansion when his father died. And originally the house was built by William Crispin III's grandfather."

Stevie let out a long, low whistle. "Whoooo! That house is really old!"

"Mansion," Laura corrected Stevie this time.

"Whatever," Stevie said. "But never mind that, take a look at *this*!" She pointed to a folded, thicker page, which she started to unfold. "Just what I thought it was," Stevie congratulated herself. "A map of the whole Crispin estate. It shows everything!"

"Look," Laura said, leaning in closer to get a better view. "There's the graveyard, and the garden, and there's even a drawing of the statue."

"And here's our Clue Club meeting place!" Molly said, getting up on her knees on the chair and leaning all the way over the map. "It's the barn!"

All the girls were busily searching out familiar points of interest on the map of the Crispin estate, when at the same time Meg and Laura saw the same thing. "What is it?" Laura asked Meg as the two traced a thick dotted line from the barn to the mansion.

"That's what I'm trying to figure out," Meg said seriously as she ran her finger over the line again. "I don't remember seeing a path like this between the barn and mansion."

"That's because there isn't one," Stevie said, adding her own finger to the line. "This isn't a path *on* the ground. I think it's a path *under* the ground!"

"You mean a tunnel, Stevie?" Molly asked, taking an even closer look until her elbows hurt from pressing so hard against the tabletop.

"But where does it start?" Laura wondered, trying to see between Meg's bouncing curls, Stevie's long strings of hair, and Molly's scrunched-up elbows.

"I don't think we can tell from the map," Meg said, studying the barn plan. "I think we're going to have to go there and see for ourselves."

"Now?" Laura asked, unable to hide the feeling of fear that suddenly overcame her as she thought of being in a tunnel.

"Now," said Meg without hesitation.

Stevie and Molly were already standing up and folding the big map back into the book. Together they lifted it back onto the book cart and wheeled it over to where Mrs. Kelly stood behind the counter.

"Find what you were looking for?" she asked the girls.

"Yes, and even something we weren't looking for!" Stevie said.

Molly hurriedly spoke up in case Stevie was going to say too much about the tunnel. "Thank you so much for getting the book. It was a big help for our . . . uh . . . project."

"I'm glad I could help." Mrs. Kelly smiled. "See you girls another day."

Laura, Meg, Molly, and Stevie quickly headed for the door. Once they were outside they all began talking excitedly at once.

"Can you believe what this might mean?" Meg said.

"Yes," answered Laura. "It might mean I'm going to be scared to death in about five minutes."

"Laura," Stevie said, putting an assuring arm around Laura's shoulders, "we'll all be together. Don't worry. And besides, what could happen?"

"We won't know that until we get there, and

we won't get there until we start going, so I say let's go!" Molly pulled Meg's sleeve. Meg reached out and held onto Stevie's sleeve. Stevie caught Laura's sleeve. Like a train on the track to a great adventure, the four girls wove their way through garden paths and backyard cut-throughs to the big iron gates of the Crispin Mansion.

It was all familiar to them now, so there was nothing to stop them from pushing right through the gates and running all the way to the barn. This time when they got there, everything was as it should have been. Nothing had been moved or rearranged. As far as they could tell, no one else had been in the barn since they were last there.

"Well, that's a relief," Laura sighed, feeling much better.

Meg was already picking up a pitchfork that leaned against a post and beginning to push aside piles of hay that covered the barn floor.

The others saw what Meg was doing and im-mediately found their own sticks, brooms, and tools to push away hay. They had cleared the whole floor, and still they couldn't find what they were looking for.

"It has to be a trapdoor in the floor," Meg

insisted. "But we've looked everywhere."

"Well, at least the barn floor is all cleaned up," laughed Molly.

"Not all," Laura's voice called out, sounding farther away than she was. "There's a closet here!" Laura stood inside a small closet that was filled with old bridles, ropes, reins, and other tack used for horseback riding.

"Wow!" Molly said, her eyes lighting up at the sight of anything to do with horses. "Look at all this stuff! How could we have missed this closet?"

"Because," Laura answered, "it wasn't here before. I was pushing the hay back against this wall, and when my broom hit the wall, the wall opened up. There's no handle on the door anymore, so we just didn't know it was a door, I guess."

The floor of the tiny closet was clear. As the four girls looked around on the shelves and finally down at their feet, they all saw the brass ring attached to the floor.

"It's the trapdoor!" Stevie shouted. "It's *got* to be!"

"Somebody pull up the ring!" Molly said excitedly. But she didn't step forward to be the first to open the trapdoor. For a minute, no one else stepped forward, either.

"Well," Laura said, "go on, get it over with. I'm getting the shivers again."

"I'll do it," Stevie said finally, leaning down and linking her index finger through the tarnished brass ring. She pulled, and with almost no effort she was able to bring up a part of the floor. The trapdoor opened all the way and fell flat back. As a little cloud of dust floated up from the floor where the door hit, four gasps escaped from the lips of the Clue Club members.

"I don't believe this!" Molly almost whispered as she peered down the dark hole.

"Believe it," said Meg, looking past Molly and even deeper down the pit in the floor. "This is exactly what was on the map. Stevie was right. It *is* a tunnel."

"Well, what are we waiting for? Let's go in." Stevie started right down the wooden stairway and stopped after taking only two steps. "Oh, I guess we need a flashlight."

"I've got one," Meg said. "It's up in the hayloft with the club stuff." She turned and ran up the stairs, found the flashlight easily, and was back down before Stevie even had a chance to get back out of the hole in the floor.

"Don't get out, Stevie," Molly said as Stevie was just about to step out. "Meg's got the flashlight."

"Great," Stevie said, taking the orange flashlight from Meg. "But you guys are coming down here with me, aren't you?" She flashed the light down the stairs, and they were all surprised to see that there were only five steps to the dirt floor.

"Well, that's a relief," Laura said for the second time that afternoon.

"What are you relieved about *this* time?" Meg asked, following Stevie down the stairs.

"That it's not some long, long stairway leading all the way to China or something," Laura explained, as she headed down the stairs after Meg.

Molly was right behind Laura. "It's long enough," she said. "And it's so dark in here."

Stevie shined the light ahead of them, and they could see more of the details of the long, dark, underground hallway. Although the floor was unfinished, with tightly packed dirt forming a hard, smooth pathway, there were walls made of raw wood timbers. It was obviously a sturdily built tunnel that had been used often in the days when the family still lived in the Crispin Mansion. Kerosene lanterns hung on wooden pegs every five feet or so, but they were empty and had no wicks. Even if the girls had matches, the lanterns would have been of no use to them.

"Well, that's a — " Laura started to say.

" — relief." Stevie, Meg, and Molly finished Laura's sentence.

Laura laughed. "Well, it *is*," she insisted. "I was afraid there would be rats or snakes or something down here. There's nothing but a bunch of — "

"Spiders!" screamed Molly, shaking her arm as fast as she could shake it to get a big black spider off. "Yeecch!" she shrieked, grabbing onto Meg's arm and causing Meg to shriek, too.

Stevie quickly wheeled around to catch the spider in the light of the flashlight. She pointed it down at the floor just in time to see the hairy thing scurry into a crevice in the timbers.

"Look!" shouted Laura, pointing down at the floor.

"It's gone, Laura," Stevie said. "It went into the crack in the wall."

"Not that," said Laura, bending down to pick something up. *"This!"* In her outstretched palm was a single rose petal. The flashlight made it clear that this rose petal was the same color as all the others.

"The Rose!" Meg said, forgetting the spider. "Now we have proof that *she* was here. And we

111

can be pretty sure she was the one who moved the club stuff around."

"And put the gown in my ballet bag," Laura added.

"And the rose in the statue's hand," said Molly.

"Let's keep going," Stevie said, turning her light ahead again. "I want to see where this thing ends up."

"I think I have an idea about that," Meg said mysteriously as they kept walking.

"So share the info," Stevie said back to her.

"Hey, look ahead!" Molly pointed at another set of stairs just like the ones they'd come down. "We're at the end!"

"And now we'll see if I was right," said Meg. "Want me to go up first this time?"

"Sure," said Stevie, handing her the light.

"No, you keep the light," Meg said. "Just shine it up the stairway so I can see at the top."

"Oh, Meg," Laura cried, "please be careful. Who knows what's waiting up there for us?"

"I'm not worried about that," Meg answered. "All I'm worried about is finding a way to open this thing up." She pushed hard in the middle. It didn't budge.

"Try on the side," Stevie suggested. "Maybe

the handle isn't the same as on the other one."

Meg gave another push, on the side this time. Immediately the square door lifted up, and Meg poked her head through the opening. "It's as dark out here as it is down there," she whispered over her shoulder, down to the other girls.

"How could it be?" Laura asked. "Isn't it inside the house?"

"It's hard to tell," Meg's muffled voice said. "Shine the light up here, can you?" Meg peered around, trying to follow the narrow beam of the flashlight. Then suddenly she shouted happily, "I was right!"

"About what?" Molly yelled up.

"Come on up, you guys. It's all right. Really." Meg climbed up the rest of the way and found herself just where she thought she would — inside of the closet in the bedroom with the canopy bed. She pushed back a rack full of old dresses and found the closet door on the other side of them. Pushing it open all the way, Meg allowed daylight to outshine the light of the flashlight.

Stevie stayed at the bottom of the stairs holding the light while Molly and then Laura climbed up and out of the tunnel. When they were safely up, Stevie followed. As she came out into the folds of more dresses than she ever cared to see in her entire lifetime, Stevie pushed her way through saying, "Ugh! Trapped in the Evil Land of Evening Wear! Why would anyone ever want so many *dresses*?"

The other girls, who were already out of the closet and standing in the middle of the room, laughed as Stevie burst through the billows of chiffon, lace, and satin.

"*I* would want so many dresses," Laura answered Stevie's question. She pushed several of the hangers along the wooden closet pole and held out the satin and lace skirt of one lilac-colored dress. "I love this one!"

"Don't even say it, Laura," warned Molly. "The next thing you know you'll find it in your ballet bag."

"Well, at least we know one thing," Meg said seriously. "It wasn't a ghost or anything too mysterious that took the dress out of the closet and put it on the bed that day."

"And it wasn't a ghost who took the dress off the bed and put it in Laura's bag, either," Stevie added.

"No, it was a real, live person," said Meg, bending down to pick up something. "And we all know who that person is." Meg held out her hand so all the others could see the rose petals she'd just picked up off the floor. There were five of them.

"The Rose," Laura said quietly.

"The Rose," Meg repeated. "Now if we could just find out *where* she is. . . ."

"I think we should leave," Laura said nervously. *"Now."*

"So do I," Molly agreed.

"I think so, too," Meg said, "but first I want to do one thing." Very carefully, Meg placed the rose petals she'd found on the bed. She arranged them in a row of four and placed the fifth one underneath the row, separate from the others.

"Why did you do that, Meg?" Laura asked.

"I just figure we might as well leave our *own* message. The Rose won't know we know about the tunnel. So she'll have a little mystery of her own to solve now," Meg explained.

"You're a genius, Meg," Molly praised her.

"But what does it mean?" asked Laura, looking at the row of four petals above the one.

"It means four is company, and five is definitely a crowd," said Meg firmly. Then she turned to Stevie and in her most official-sounding Clue Club voice she said, "Stevie, lead the way!"

"Sir, yes sir!" said Stevie, clicking her heels together and saluting Meg.

The passage through the tunnel was faster this time, and no spiders tried to hitch a ride on any of them. Still, they were happy to reach the staircase at the end, and follow the beam of light from the orange flashlight out into the tiny closet. When all of them were safely out of the tunnel and the big trapdoor was closed they all felt better. Molly giggled nervously. Meg put a hand over her heart and breathed out so hard the curl on her forehead flew up. Stevie fell back dramatically against the wall and slid down to a deep knee bend. And Laura just blinked her eyes and said quietly, "Well, that's a relief!"

THE LUNCHEON

When Laura and Molly met on the corner, they both held a note in their hands. Laura's note was from Meg and it read:

Dear Laura,
Dance, dance, dance
In your rose gown so fair,
And always remember

Your best friends will be there!
Good luck today!

Your Friend 4-Ever,

Meg

Molly's note was from Stevie, and Molly couldn't help but laugh when she read it aloud to Laura. "Listen to this," she said.

Dear Molly,
Put your ballet shoes
On your feet today
And put your cowgirl
Boots away.
Point your toes
And dance your best,
And give those cowgirl
Boots a rest!

Yours 'til the kitchen sinks,

STEVIE

Both Laura and Molly had checked their Secret Note Society hiding places on their way to meet each other before the ballet performance at Mrs. Crispin's house. This was the big day and both girls felt nervous, even though they knew their parts perfectly. Stevie's funny little poem was exactly what they needed to break the tension.

"I don't know why I feel so nervous," Laura admitted to Molly. "I couldn't even sleep last night. I kept getting up and looking at that gown hanging on my closet door. It's as if it was staring at me all night or something."

Molly laughed. "A dress staring at you? *Now* I've heard everything!" Then when she saw the troubled look on her friend's face, Molly got serious. "Oh, Laura," she said, "are you sure you want to wear it?"

"I have to. I promised Mrs. Crispin I would. And besides, I'm not going to let a silly dress ruin one of the most exciting days of my life." Laura held her head up and looked like she'd made up her mind. Molly didn't say any more. Even if she'd wanted to, the arrival of Stevie and Meg would have interrupted her.

"Hi, guys!" Stevie called out. "How do I look?" Stevie did a clumsy model's turn so everyone could see that she, Stevie Ames, was actually, really and truly wearing a dress.

"You look beautiful!" Laura said as Stevie held out the red-and-white-striped skirt of the sundress.

"Yeah, it's about the only thing I have that my brothers didn't wear first!" Stevie laughed. "It isn't the real me, but I have to wear it for the luncheon."

"I got your note," Laura said, turning the attention to Meg. "Thanks."

"And I got yours, too," said Meg happily, holding up a unicorn-decorated note that simply said,

Dear Meg,
I've got to go.
I'll talk to you
After the show!

                   Friends 4-Ever and ever,

                        Laura

"Me, too," Stevie said, holding up her rainbow-covered note. "Short but sweet," she added because her note was only two lines:

Dear Stevie,
Yikes! I'm soooo nervous.
Wish me luck!
                    Your friend with the jitters,

Molly

Once all the notes were shared, the girls paired off. Molly and Stevie walked side by side, and Meg and Laura led the way arm in arm. Miss Humphrey had told all the girls to be at her studio by ten-thirty. The plan was that she would give them some last minute instructions, check that they had their costumes in order, and then she would drive them all over in her big blue van. The teacher had agreed to take Stevie and Meg along, too.

"I know exactly what she's going to say,"

Molly whispered to Laura as they stood in a line with the rest of the dancers waiting for Miss Humphrey to speak.

"Heads held high!" began the teacher dramatically as she waved her arms above her head.

"I knew she was going to say that," Molly giggled into Laura's ear.

"Walk tall, dance proudly! First stop Camden. Next stop — "

"Broadway!" both Molly and Miss Humphrey said it together.

"Yes, Miss Molly," said Miss Humphrey, smiling at the student who had obviously listened well. "Broadway. Now, let me say one final thing. I know you will all show me what kind of stars you are — not falling stars, but rising ones! Into the van, stars. Into the van!"

Scarves waving, bracelets jangling, Miss Humphrey led the group of dancers to the van. The next stop was not Broadway. It was Mrs. Crispin's huge house, high on a hill on the other side of town.

As the group piled out, the first thing the four friends noticed was the walkway leading to the towering double doors. It was exactly the same as the walkway at the old Crispin Mansion. The stones were laid out in the same diagonal pattern, and the path was outlined with beautiful white rose bushes.

"Remind you of any place?" Stevie murmured to Meg.

"I'll say," Meg answered in the same low voice.

"It's just like the other Crispin Mansion!" Molly came up behind them, whispering.

"That's what we were just saying," Meg started to explain, but she stopped because both front doors swung open. Standing there to greet the group, Mrs. Crispin welcomed the girls into the great marble foyer of the biggest house Meg, Molly, Stevie, and Laura had ever been inside.

"Wow!" gasped Laura as she turned a full circle looking up at the cathedral ceiling and the dazzling crystal chandelier that hung down from it.

"You can say that again!" said Stevie. "It's like Cinderella's castle or something!"

"Ladies," Mrs. Crispin was saying to the group, "welcome to Crispin Manor. I'm so pleased that you're here, and I know your ballet performance is going to be wonderful. You may all go into the room off the ballroom to get ready. Miss Humphrey will be able to answer any questions you have, while I attend to the final details with the caterers who are serving the food. But please, make yourselves comfortable. And try to think of my home as your home."

"I wouldn't have to try very hard," Stevie joked to Meg. "I could go home and pack up my stuff to move in here in a minute!"

"Me, too," said Meg, watching the dancers follow Miss Humphrey through the doors that led to the spacious ballroom and to another room off it. "But where are *we* supposed to go, I wonder? And what is the job she has for us?"

Stevie didn't wait for Mrs. Crispin to come to them. She boldly walked up to the white-haired woman and spoke. "Hi, Mrs. Crispin! Remember me? Stevie Ames."

"Yes! Yes, of course," replied Mrs. Crispin. "And here's Meg, too. I'm so glad the two of you could come to help out today. I am so eager for you to — " She stopped talking when one of the waitresses came to her with a question about where to set up the dessert table.

"Will you excuse me for a minute, girls?" she said to Stevie and Meg. "I have to see to this matter, but please do some more exploring if you like and I'll speak to you in a little while." She followed the waitress into the ballroom

124

where the luncheon tables were already set up. Stevie and Meg could see the beautiful white linen tablecloths and bowls of white roses on each table.

Finding themselves left alone, the girls decided to walk around and do just what Mrs. Crispin suggested, explore. First they looked in a room on the left of the foyer. It was a parlor room, with leather wing chairs set in front of a large marble fireplace. Over the mantle there hung a full-length portrait of Mrs. Crispin at a much younger age. Her hair was brown instead of white and flowed down her back and over her shoulders.

"Wasn't she so pretty?" Meg said admiringly. "Her face really hasn't changed very much."

"Yeah," agreed Stevie. "But her hair has. I wonder if it's still so long."

Meg was already off exploring another part of the room. She stood before a closed door and turned the handle. "Stevie!" she whispered loudly. "Come here! It's a bedroom."

"It looks more like a museum room or something," Stevie said, peering into a large bedroom that looked like it was never used. The brocade bedspread was pulled tightly over the perfectly puffed pillows. An old book lay open on the night table, and a pair of wire-framed glasses sat on the book.

"It's just a little too perfect, even for me," Meg said.

"I could fix that in a minute." Stevie laughed, thinking of the mess her room usually was.

"Never mind that," Meg said. "Let's keep going. I hear some of the guests arriving, and I want to see more before we have to sit down." She walked across the room and through another doorway. This one led to a glass atrium filled with beautiful ferns in all shades of green.

"It's like a jungle room," Stevie said, walking through the leafy plants. "I almost expect to see a tiger or an elephant or . . . Meg! Look!" Stevie was standing in yet another doorway, and she wasn't moving.

Meg hurried over to the spot where Stevie stood. Her mouth fell open almost as wide as Stevie's. There before them was a glassed-in area big enough to be called a house.

"A greenhouse!" Meg gasped. "And it's full of roses!"

"Not just roses, Meg," Stevie added. "The Rose's roses!"

The greenhouse was filled with nothing but roses in colors the girls had never seen before. One species of rose stood out to them. It was the same color as all the roses that had become a part of their lives since that first time in the Yellow Brick Road restaurant.

"I don't get it," Meg said, looking totally baffled. "How could this be? Is Mrs. Crispin The Rose?"

"Maybe we've had it all wrong all this time," Stevie added. "But why would an old lady want to . . . and how would she . . . ?"

"Stevie! We've got to go now! I don't want her to find us in here. Come on!" Meg pushed Stevie out the door, back through the atrium, through the bedroom, through the parlor room, and out into the foyer again. They could hear the talking and laughter of the luncheon crowd who were already finding their tables in the ballroom.

Just as Meg and Stevie were about to enter the ballroom to find Mrs. Crispin, they heard the sound of glass shattering in the parlor room.

"Gosh, I hope we didn't break something on our way through there," Meg said, looking concerned.

"There goes our allowance for the next billion years if we did," moaned Stevie. "We'd better see what it is and hope it isn't some antique vase or something."

The girls timidly poked their heads back into

the parlor to see what had broken. Right away they saw the pieces of a small china candy dish on the floor by the fireplace, and a girl bent over hurrying to pick them up. She heard Stevie and Meg come in, and looked up.

"You!" Stevie said, astonished, as she stood looking into the face of the girl the Clue Club had been trying to find for the past two weeks.

The girl stood up and was speechless. She seemed as surprised to see Stevie and Meg as they were to see her.

"What are you doing — ?" Before Meg could finish her sentence, another voice spoke.

"Oh, there you are!" Mrs. Crispin said. "And I see you've found Rose."

"You know about The Rose?" both girls said together. They couldn't believe it. First they'd found the rare roses. Now they'd found the strange girl.

"Why, of course I know Rose," laughed Mrs. Crispin, putting an arm around the shoulder of the girl in glasses. "She's my granddaughter."

Meg and Stevie exchanged looks of surprise. Stevie was just about to open her mouth and let out a stream of questions, when Mrs. Crispin pulled her granddaughter forward, and said, "Rose, I'd like you to meet — "

"Stevie and Meg," the girl finished her grand-mother's sentence.

"Oh!" said a surprised Mrs. Crispin. "I guess you've already introduced yourselves. Well, that's wonderful, because what I wanted you two girls to do today was join Rose at a table for the ballet performance so she wouldn't be stuck sitting with a bunch of elderly ladies."

So that was the "job" Mrs. Crispin had in mind for them, thought Stevie. Sitting with the girl who had been following the Friends 4-Ever and spying on them for the past couple of weeks! There was no chance to object. The sound of applause and the first notes of the opening music reached them from the ballroom.

"Oh, my!" said Mrs. Crispin. "We'd better hurry along now. I have a table for you girls right in the front." Without another moment's hesitation, Mrs. Crispin hurried the girls out of the parlor. She never even mentioned the broken candy dish. But she did take Meg aside and whispered, "Do be friendly to Rose, won't you, dear? She needs some friends her own age. I'll explain later."

Meg and Stevie were not too happy with the situation. In fact, they were still in a state of shock at the whole turn of events. As they both

129

pulled out a chair on either side of the girl named Rose, they looked over her head at each other and shook their heads from side to side.

"Wait 'til Laura and Molly see this!" Stevie silently mouthed to Meg.

"I think they just did," Meg mouthed back.

Sure enough, from their spots in the center of the stage area, Laura and Molly stood motionless as their eyes found The Rose sitting right between their two friends. If Molly hadn't given her a little push, Laura might have missed her first step leading the Lilies and Daffodils through the painted garden scenery. The music carried Laura across the stage, but her eyes never left the eyes of The Rose.

ROSE

Stevie and Meg had trouble concentrating on the dance performance. Throughout the entire program, they watched Rose watching Laura. The girl hadn't said a word to them yet, and until intermission Meg and Stevie couldn't begin asking her the thousands of questions they had ready for her. Stevie looked over at Meg and rolled her eyes upward.

Meg rolled her eyes back at Stevie, and behind Rose's back she mouthed the words, "We *have* to be nice."

Stevie shook her head defiantly and folded her

arms stubbornly over her chest. "*I* don't," she mouthed.

"We *both* do," Meg mouthed back.

Rose couldn't see the girls' mouths moving, but she must have sensed the conversation going on behind her. She turned her attention from Laura to Meg and Stevie. The light from the foyer bounced off Rose's glasses, allowing Stevie to see her own reflection. Her face looked angry. So did Meg's. Neither one of them felt a bit like being nice to the girl who had been the cause of so much worry. Stevie made up her mind right then and there that no explanation the girl could give would be enough of an excuse. There *was* no excuse for making Laura feel afraid.

As if she had heard Stevie thinking, Rose turned her eyes back to Laura and then back to Stevie. In the semidarkness she whispered, "She's the most beautiful dancer I've ever, ever seen."

Onstage, Laura tried hard to keep her head held high. Looking straight ahead, the hot spotlights weren't the only things she could feel on her. From that table in the front where the strange girl sat, she could feel the girl's eyes following every move she made. How did she even get here? Laura wondered. And why in the world was she sitting with Stevie and Meg? It was all she could do to keep her concentration on the dance she was supposed to be starring in. It was only with Molly's help and the memory of Miss Humphrey's voice saying, *The show must go on! Let nothing distract you. Look out above the audience, not into it!* that Laura was able to finish the first half of the performance. As she took her bow, the audience applauded with great appreciation. But one person seemed to be clapping harder and louder than anyone else. Rose was up out of her chair, standing in the same trance-like manner as she had in the restaurant. Her eyes were glued to Laura.

"That does it," Stevie said aloud. Her words were drowned out by the applause, but she wasn't about to wait a minute longer. She flashed Meg an angry look that seemed to say, "Let's get her!" Meg returned the look.

Both girls were about to lean over and bombard Rose with questions when Mrs. Crispin came up behind them and put one hand on Stevie's shoulder and another on Meg's. "Isn't it a wonderful program?" she said, loud enough for them to hear over the applause.

The hand on her shoulder caused Stevie to jump a little. "Oh, Mrs. Crispin!" she sputtered in surprise.

"I'm sorry. I didn't mean to startle you, dear,"

the hostess apologized. "I just wanted to see how you're all getting along." Before she could say any more, the music began again, and the intermission was over. The second half of the program began.

Mrs. Crispin left the girls to take her seat at another table. Stevie and Meg watched her go, and once again were left with The Rose.

Rose didn't seem to notice her grandmother's coming or going. Her dark eyes could only see Laura standing in the center of the stage wearing the rose-colored gown. The music for *The Dance of the Rose* started out softly. Laura stood with her arms in a circle out in front of her waist. Her head was bowed down. As the sound of the violins swelled, Laura slowly lifted her eyes, then her whole head, until she stood straight and tall, looking out above the audience. The crash of cymbals signaled her to leap gracefully across the stage, weaving in and out of the Lilies and Daffodils as she made her way back to the center. In the background the Lilies and Daffodils swayed and dipped and did their best to shine as Molly and Laura filled the main spotlight.

Finally the stringed instruments quieted, and the dancers returned to their original positions in the painted garden scenery. Laura and Molly were the only dancers moving as they swirled around each other in the last moments of the dance. A flute played, and this was Molly's cue to open her arms behind Laura, a rainbow framing a beautiful rose.

"This is my favorite part," Meg whispered to Stevie. "Doesn't Laura look incredibly beautiful in that dress?"

"You're not the only one who thinks so," Stevie whispered back, pointing her thumb at Rose.

Meg looked over at the girl and was surprised to see tears rolling down Rose's cheeks as she watched Laura. Meg looked over at Stevie to see if she noticed the tears, too. Meg pointed them out to her.

Stevie did an exaggerated double take. "What?" she barely whispered. "What's she crying for?" Stevie didn't get it at all. It was a pretty dance and all, but hardly worth crying over.

Even though Stevie had whispered, Rose heard her. She quickly reached a hand up to her face and wiped the tears away, but more fell. If it hadn't been so dark in the big ballroom, Meg and Stevie would have seen the blush of embarrassment spread across Rose's face. Instead, all they saw was Rose suddenly stand up, just as the ballet ended, and turn and run out of the room. As she pushed past table after table of applauding luncheon guests, Stevie and Meg stood up, too. Laura and Molly were taking their bows. Still standing, Stevie and Meg applauded louder than any of the other guests. As soon as the last bow was taken, they signaled Laura and Molly, pointing to the doorway to show that they were going after the runaway girl.

Now, Meg and Stevie were the ones making their way through the rows of tables and chairs to the doorway. Once out in the marble foyer, they looked both ways and didn't see a sign of Rose.

"Let's try the parlor room," Meg said, heading across the floor to the room where they'd first found Rose.

"Not here," Stevie reported after a quick look around. "Keep going. She couldn't have gotten too far."

The two girls were just heading into the adjoining bedroom when Molly and Laura came running in, still wearing their costumes. "Did you get her?" Laura asked hopefully. "How did she get into Mrs. Crispin's house?"

"She's even sneakier than we thought!" Molly added.

"She didn't sneak in," Meg told them. "Mrs. Crispin is her grandmother!"

"I don't believe it!" Laura gasped. "The Rose is Mrs. Crispin's granddaughter?"

"And The Rose really is named Rose," Stevie said. "The job Mrs. Crispin had for us was to baby-sit The Rose. Can you believe after all this, that Rose is — "

"Oh, there you girls are!" Mrs. Crispin's voice interrupted Stevie. "And Rose will be so — " The white-haired woman stopped. "But where is Rose?" she asked, seeing that her grand-daughter was missing.

"Good question, Mrs. Crispin," Stevie answered. "She just ran out and we don't know where she went."

"I'm afraid she was crying, Mrs. Crispin," Meg said, feeling a little guilty since it had been their job to look after the girl.

"Oh, dear," said Mrs. Crispin, biting her lower lip a little. "Poor little Rose. It's all been so difficult for her."

"Difficult for *her*?" Stevie blurted out. "What about for Laura? Laura's the one who was being spied on and followed and scared to death by Rose."

Molly gave Stevie a big nudge with her elbow

and hissed a *"Sshhh!"* at her. But it was too late. Mrs. Crispin already looked surprised, concerned, and curious.

"What do you mean, Stevie dear?" she said, putting a hand up to her pearl necklace.

Before Stevie could answer, Laura started explaining for herself what had been going on for the past two weeks. She told about the first time they saw Rose at the Yellow Brick Road restaurant. She told about the rose that Rose handed to Laura and the one she left in the hand of the statue at the Crispin Mansion garden. Mrs. Crispin listened closely as Laura went on to tell her about the note and rose petals in her Secret Note hiding place, and finally about the rose-colored gown that suddenly showed up in her ballet bag.

Now that Laura had mentioned the garden at the Crispin Mansion and the dress that had been inside the house, Meg thought it was a good time to tell about the Clue Club meeting in Mrs. Crispin's barn. When she'd finished explaining why they needed a meeting place of their own and how Stevie had discovered the barn while she was up high in her climbing tree, Mrs. Crispin smiled and shook her head.

"Well, I certainly understand a lot of things

now that I didn't understand before," she said thoughtfully.

"And I don't understand *anything*," Molly said, flipping back her rainbow cape. "Like first of all where did she go?"

Mrs. Crispin spoke quietly. "I think I have an idea where Rose is. But before we go to her I'd like to talk with you girls a little." The stately woman took a deep breath and sat down in one of the leather wing chairs. "Please sit down here around me, if you don't mind."

Meg sat right down with her legs folded to the side. She smoothed her light blue dress out over her legs, and waited for the others to be seated, too. Stevie plopped down next to Meg. Even though she wore a dress, Stevie sat cross-legged and then tried to pull the red-and-white-striped skirt over her knees. Laura and Molly sat a little more carefully so they wouldn't tear their delicate costumes.

"Thank you, girls," said Mrs. Crispin when they were all settled. "Now let me tell you about my granddaughter, Rose. I'm afraid she's been a very unhappy girl."

"Why?" Stevie asked, anxious to hear it all immediately.

"Well, I suppose it has been hard for her to

move from place to place, never having a chance to stay anywhere long enough to make real friends. My son and his wife are in the theater. They are actors in a theater company that travels all around this country and Europe."

"Europe!" Stevie exclaimed. "Wow! And Rose goes with them? Wouldn't that be so incredible? I've never been anywhere except Kansas!"

"Well, dear" — Mrs. Crispin smiled — "it might not seem so appealing if you never really had a place to call home. Of course, Mr. Crispin was so disappointed when our son, Charles, decided not to go into the banking business as his father and grandfather had done. But this was his choice and he and Marta are very happy. They've always loved bringing Rose along everywhere they go, and Rose was happy to go until recently. It seems now she's missing having friends."

"That must be why she's been following us," Meg said, beginning to understand a little. "Maybe she just wanted to be friends with us."

"Well, that's a strange way to make friends, spying on us, I mean," Stevie said with annoyance.

"Oh, I'm sure she never meant to spy, Stevie. Perhaps she was just watching to see how — "

Another voice finished the sentence. " — to see how real friends act."

The girls looked up from their places on the floor and saw that it was Rose speaking from the doorway leading to the bedroom.

"Rose, dear," said Mrs. Crispin, holding out her arms to the girl. "Won't you come here?"

Tears dripped slowly from behind the glasses that framed her black-brown eyes, and she did not move forward. She stood looking down at her feet. "I'm sorry," she whispered. "I'm sorry for everything. You were right. It was me who did all the things you said I did. But I wasn't trying to scare anyone. Especially not you, Laura." The girl looked up and right at Laura, who now had tears in her eyes, too.

"Yeah, why Laura?" Stevie wanted to know.

"I think I can answer that," Mrs. Crispin said softly. "It was *The Dance of the Rose*, wasn't it, dear?" she said kindly to Rose.

Rose shook her head up and down and sniffled a little. Laura reached into her sleeve and pulled out a white handkerchief embroidered with tiny rosebuds. She stood up gracefully and walked over to where Rose was standing. "Here," she said sweetly. "Take this, please." Laura put the handkerchief in Rose's hand.

"Thank you," Rose said quietly.

Stevie had no patience for this scene. She wanted to hear more. "Well, what about *The Dance of the Rose*?" she asked Mrs. Crispin. "What does that have to do with anything?"

"*The Dance of the Rose* is the dance that Rose herself was supposed to do in a performance given by her parents' theater company. It was going to be a very special event, and Rose was selected from hundreds of girls. But the day of the opening performance she couldn't seem to find the courage."

"I was too afraid," Rose said angrily. "I knew I'd never be as good a dancer as you were, Grandmother, and as my mother is. I knew I would just disappoint everyone. I couldn't do it. I'm just too shy."

A light seemed to go on in Molly's head. "Just like Laura is!" she said.

For a second, Rose's face almost looked happy. "Yes," she said, relieved that someone finally seemed to be understanding her a little. "When I saw Laura on the stage at the recital, dancing in front of everyone and not looking a bit scared, I thought she was the most wonderful girl in the whole world."

"Well, you're right about that," Meg said,

warming up to the girl just a little.

"I knew I could never be like Laura," Rose continued shyly, "but I hoped I could somehow be her friend." Rose looked down at her feet again, feeling embarrassed and shy in front of the girls she'd watched only from a distance until now.

Mrs. Crispin got up to put a comforting arm around Rose. As she stood patting her granddaughter on the shoulder, the same waitress who had asked her questions earlier came looking for her. "Mrs. Crispin?" said the young woman. "You are needed in the ballroom. The luncheon is to be served in a moment."

"Oh dear," said Mrs. Crispin, suddenly realizing that she'd been away from her own party too long. "Will you excuse me, dears? I'm sorry to leave you like this, but we'll continue later." Apologizing again, she hurried out with the waitress following her, leaving the five girls alone in the parlor.

The four Friends 4-Ever stood together and apart from Rose. The way they were standing reminded Meg of the rose petal message she'd left on the bed in the room of the old Crispin Mansion. Four petals and one extra. Seeing Rose standing alone and looking friendless, Meg hoped the girl had not gone back through the secret tunnel. In spite of what Rose had done, Meg suddenly stopped seeing her as a mysterious stranger. Now she saw her as just a lonely little girl, no different from the rest of them really, except that the rest of them had friends.

Stevie and Molly began to see the same thing when they looked at Rose. And then Stevie tried to lighten the seriousness of the moment by joking, "I guess picking roses is easier than picking friends!"

Rose blushed at the mention of the roses. Laura stepped away from the other girls and put an arm around Rose's shoulders. "She's just joking," Laura explained gently.

"I picked the rose to give to you at the recital," Rose defended herself. "But I was afraid you'd think I was silly since you didn't even know me."

"No, I wouldn't have thought that," Laura said.

"She wouldn't," echoed Molly.

"Then you all went to the Yellow Brick Road, so I went there, too."

"And you brought the rose with you, right?" Stevie said.

"Yes," Rose answered.

144

"And you gave it to Laura, and then you disappeared," Molly added.

"Well, I didn't really disappear," Rose explained. "I just hid behind the jukebox. Then I overheard all the things you said about starting the Clue Club to find me. I've never been in a club before. I never lived any place long enough to start one or join one. I saw what good friends you all are, and I knew I'd probably never be able to be in your club. So I thought the next best thing was to at least have your club keep trying to find me. Do you know what I mean? I just wanted to be a part of it all." Tears were in her eyes again. And this time she just let them fall. No one said a word, and when she finally looked up at the girls, Rose was surprised to see their tears through her own.

"I'm really sorry," she said again. "I was only trying to — "

Rose didn't have a chance to finish her sentence. Right at that awkward moment, Miss Humphrey breezed into the room like a gust of wind with her headdress of colorful scarves blowing out behind her.

"Ah! There are my stars!" the overly made-up teacher bellowed in her best stage voice. "Marvelous! You were both marvelous! Definitely

Broadway bound! In fact, I wondered if you'd already packed your things and headed that way. All the girls have been looking for you. You ran off even before the final, final bow." Her bracelets clinked and clanked as she gave her hands a couple of quick hurry-along-now claps. "The luncheon is being served now and the food looks — "

"Good enough to eat?" Stevie finished for her.

Stevie's joke broke the tension of the moment. All the girls laughed.

"Exactly!" Miss Humphrey said, pointing one finger up in the air to punctuate her word. "Let's go back to the ballroom now. Dancers must eat, too. And I've arranged it so your friends can sit with the dancer group, too," she said to Laura and Molly.

"Us?" Meg asked, meaning Stevie and her.

"Why, all three of you, of course," Miss Humphrey said, looking at Rose, too.

Rose started to protest, sure that the other girls wouldn't want anything to do with her after all the trouble she had caused them. "Oh, no, that's all right. I'll just sit with my — "

"Friends," said Laura, smiling at the girl and putting out a hand to shake on it.

Seeing Laura make the first move, the others

followed her lead. First Molly stuck out her hand to shake with Rose, then Stevie, then Meg. "Friends," they said as Rose accepted each hand.

Suddenly Stevie announced that she was starved.

"Me, too," Molly said.

"Me three," Meg added.

"Me four," Laura said.

"Me five," Rose said with a shy smile.

Arm in arm the four friends plus one headed back to the ballroom where the tables were piled high with tea sandwiches, chicken croquettes, Jell-O salads, and breads and rolls of all kinds. After stacking their plates with food, the girls celebrated the success of the dance performance and the solving of the mystery of The Rose.

Before saying good-bye to Mrs. Crispin and Rose, it was decided that Rose would meet them at the Clue Club meeting place the next morning. Only this time she wouldn't have to hide. Laura, Molly, Meg, and Stevie all agreed that Rose was welcome to join the Friends 4-Ever. And from now on, Rose was to think of their club as *her* club.

The four girls waved good-bye to Rose as they drove off in Miss Humphrey's blue van. "See you tomorrow, Rose!"

Rose stood smiling and waving back from the doorway of the huge mansion.

Early the next morning, Laura, Meg, Molly, and Stevie stood at the barn door waiting for Rose. After all, it was their rule: No one goes in until everyone in the club is there. The girls waited. And they waited. No Rose.

"I'm sure she'll be here in a minute," Laura said. "Why don't we walk around in the garden until she gets here? Now that we saw the portrait of Mrs. Crispin when she was younger, it makes me think maybe the statue in the garden is of her."

"Hey, yeah!" Stevie said excitedly. "Maybe you're right! Let's go look!"

They looked up the path one more time for Rose, then ran across the grounds to the garden where the statue was. Molly galloped. Stevie ran. Meg bounced. And Laura leaped through the air and was first to reach the statue. She stopped suddenly and gasped at what she saw.

Molly, Stevie, and Meg caught up, and they, too, stopped suddenly. "What the . . . ?" Stevie said, seeing what Laura and the others also saw. It was a rose. A rare rose in the hand of the statue. And with the rose there was a note. Laura walked over, took the rose and the note from the statue's hand, and unfolded it to read aloud to the others.

> Dear Friends 4-Ever,
>   I'm sorry I couldn't come to the meeting. My parents came back last night to get me. I guess we'll be going to Europe again so I won't be able to come to the next meetings, either. But this time when I am away and in strange new places I'll always be happy because now I have some real friends. Thanks for everything. I hope you'll be my friends forever.
>
>   Not "The Rose,"
>   just Rose

Laura stood holding the note and looked up at the statue. Up close it was plain to see that it was a statue of Mrs. Crispin when she was younger. And now Laura could also see a similarity between the face of the statue and the face of Rose.

"What is it, Laura?" Meg asked quietly.

Laura smiled. "It's just that, well, all this time I was wishing I'd never heard of The Rose. And now that she's gone I think I'm going to miss her."

"It is kind of strange," Molly agreed. "She's gone just as suddenly as she got here."

Stevie moved over next to Laura and read over her shoulder. " *'Thanks for everything. I hope you'll be my friends forever,' *" she read aloud.

"I've got an idea!" Laura said suddenly.

"Hey, that's my job," joked Meg.

"What, Laura?" asked Molly.

"Let's write back to her. We'll send her a special box of stationery and then she can write back to us!" Laura's eyes shone with excitement.

"Back to the barn!" Meg announced officially as she led all the girls to the Club meeting place.

Once upstairs Meg pounded her old hammer on the hay bale table. "Order! Order!" she called out to the excited group as she took out a piece of Laura's stationery. "Laura, I think you should be the one to write this letter." She passed the unicorn paper over to Laura.

"What will I say?" Laura started. "Never mind. I know." For the next few minutes the others were quiet while Laura bent over the paper and wrote. When she was finished she read it aloud.

Dear Rose,
    Remember me when this you see,
    Remember we will always be
    Your friends forever, four plus one,
    We'll count you in on all our fun.
            Yours 'til the banana splits,
            Laura, Stevie, Molly, and Meg

"Perfect!" said Meg.

"Perfect," agreed Molly and Stevie together.

Laura stuck her right hand out. Meg's hand topped Laura's, Molly's topped Meg's, and Stevie's finished the pile.

"Friends 4-Ever," the girls said solemnly together.

"Forever," Laura whispered.

When Know-It-All Erica Soames comes to stay with the Quindlens, can Molly keep her favorite time of year from being ruined? Read Friends 4-Ever #9, C U WHEN THE SNOW FALLS.

APPLE PAPERBACKS

THE GYMNASTS™

by Elizabeth Levy